ON THE CLOCK

CLAIRE BAGLIN
ON THE CLOCK

translated from the French
by Jordan Stump

A New Directions Paperbook Original

Originally published by Les Editions de Minuit in 2022 as *En Salle*.
Published by arrangement with Les Editions de Minuit, Paris,
the Georges Borchardt Agency, New York, and Daunt Books, London.

Manufactured in the United States of America
First published as New Directions Paperbook 1624 in 2025

Library of Congress Cataloging-in-Publication Data
Names: Baglin, Claire, 1998- author. | Stump, Jordan, 1959- translator.
Title: On the clock / Claire Baglin ; translated by Jordan Stump.
Other titles: En salle. English
Description: First edition. | New York : New Directions Publishing, 2025.
Identifiers: LCCN 2024052375 | ISBN 9780811239356 (paperback) |
ISBN 9780811239363 (ebook)
Subjects: LCGFT: Novels
Classification: LCC PQ2702.A338 E513 2025 |
DDC 843/.92--dc23/eng/20241108
LC record available at https://lccn.loc.gov/2024052375

10 9 8 7 6 5 4 3 2 1

New Directions Books are published for James Laughlin
by New Directions Publishing Corporation
80 Eighth Avenue, New York 10011

ON THE CLOCK

... on the clock

THE INTERVIEW

—AND WHY here rather than elsewhere? I imagine you've applied all over, even at the competition.

The car slows down, my father hits the left blinker.

At long last, after an hour of negotiations, the van drives through the entrance, circles the parking lot a few times, and pulls to a stop. My father's keys are still in the Berlingo's ignition when mama turns around to face us. She's going to give us a warning, we're going inside but this is a special occasion and just you make sure you don't run, you don't yell. The back door has already slid open, we're outside, Nico is running, pulling his coat on one arm at a time. His shoelaces are undone, he untied them a few hours earlier, after the third highway rest stop. We have to hurry, before the parents change their minds, before they reconsider and come after us. The lamps seem to light up as we approach.

Very quickly, Nico leaves me far behind, I keep my eye on the door. My nose runs into my mouth, tears fill my ears. The glowing logo promises me they're open, it reassures me. It says we'll never let you down, we'll always be here for you, everywhere. I place all my faith in that light, which flickers every now and then.

Nico climbs the steps, his right foot catches on the last one and his face crashes into the glass door. He's laughing when I catch up with him, his nose flattened. The parents are still far behind us. Mama is untying the sleeves knotted around her waist to put on her cardigan. My father clicks the remote to lock the car doors, presses the button once, twice.

Nico shouts at them, hurry up hurry up, the fried smell comes to us through the door, the smell of celebration, the smell of the parents' surrender.

—No, no, I know your chain best. I've never tried the others.

We go inside and things get complicated. Oof, the people. The lobby's packed, we don't know where to order. It's a Sunday evening, end of the holiday. Mama says wait here but it's too late, Nico's already off. He worms his way through the crowd, shoves bodies aside with his little hands, collides with legs and dangling purses. Nico plunges into every gap and I follow after him, shrinking myself down to his size, knees bent, arms straight at my sides. I keep moving, but unlike him I apologize because we're three years apart. Nico finds an empty space and leaps through it, breaking free of the crowd. The fluorescent lights shine down on him, at last he reaches the counter. They send him back to stand in line with his parents.

Think about what you want to order while you're waiting. Nico kicks at balled-up napkins. Sometimes he gets too close to the couple in front of us, as if he's hoping to change families, and mama's fingernails claw him back. I stare gravely at the key chain on a backpack. My father's unbuttoned his jacket, he kneads his cross-body bag and frets, I don't see anything, where are the fries? is the price the one on the left or the one on the right? Mama looks around as if she'd lost someone. The corners of her mouth are scarlet from salty potato chips. When the key chain moves forward and I don't she gives me a push with her right hand. On the wall I see the new sign forbidding smoking, I read it down to the tiny letters.

At the counter, a lady in a black cap asks four questions that my father answers, well what have you got? He turns to mama, who shrugs. Nico just smiles. Then my father prods me with a glance, I have to make up my mind. On the signs, the burgers and combo meals are all new to me, the drinks twinkle. My father repeats every question the cashier asks, drink? dessert? side? I end up with a kid's meal and a glow-in-the-dark alien.

Once we're past the terror of ordering, Nico and I watch it all being made behind the counter, sometimes yelling out it's that one, it's that one, and finally my father's turn comes. He says well, well, and ends up asking for fries. The cashier pounces, she's going to eat him alive. She offers him the large Coke, the burger that's perfect when you're hungry, and my father answers how big is it? He tries to fend her off with his wallet, but how much does it cost? oh well, maybe not that then. The lady won't let him go, if you have it as part of a combo, you'll get it all for under ten euros. My father's eyes widen, the burgers are glistening too brightly for him, he's just about to surrender but makes one last stab at resistance, can I get the normal size? Mama yawns and looks at her watch, which is running slow.

—You're sure you can get up early? Your alarm clock's going to work?

The boss asks three times, maybe four, and I find myself sincerely wondering. Will I really wake up, can I promise? The boss is sitting across from me with his thirty-something face and his discreet mustache, the kind they let you have in food service. He looks at me wryly, waiting for an unrehearsed answer. He wants to know who I am and what I'm prepared to do for the sake of being on time. He's expecting me to talk about the honor of joining a team, about an interest in, about a talent for. On his sheet he's started a list, four lines, that's me. He's added a new dash, I have to give him something, and just as I'm delivering an impassioned condemnation of sleep he tries to catch me off guard.

5

—Okay, so you don't like sleeping in, but wouldn't you like to go to the seaside this summer? Enjoy your vacation?

—Yes, we take holiday vouchers, monsieur.

Jérôme flashes a quick smile of relief and opens the zipper of his bag. For a moment he'd pictured the children in tears, his wife saying what's your problem Jérôme, you could have asked earlier. He'd been dreading the return to the car, Nico threatening never to eat again as long as he lives and it'll all be your fault, then exploding into sobs at the mere thought of going one more hour without food. He'd imagined driving in complete silence, not turning on the radio, which would be taken as nothing short of a provocation. The silence would have kept up all the way into the kitchen, the children would have gulped big glasses of water to choke down the broccoli, and that would forever be what disappointment tastes like for them.

Then Sylvie would have gone to sleep on the couch after finishing off the night like you finish off an animal at the end of its life, all right time for bed you have school tomorrow.

—What are you studying? So you'll be leaving like everyone else when the fall semester starts, right?

The boss looks unhappy. When I answer, his smile comes back. At the top of his sheet, he writes mid-September and circles it twice. I'm not just dynamic, motivated, and adaptable like everyone else. Mid-September becomes my foremost quality. My application will go on the top of the pile, ahead of the wafflers, the ones who vaguely said they'd be leaving at the end of the summer vacation. I feel like the interview's nearing its end, in a moment he'll be putting a cap on my head and introducing me to my new colleagues, but I sense that convincing him will take one last touch. The pen he's holding between his fingers spins around, counting down, and a family walks past our table, balancing trays. The children pop balloons and want to go on the slide. I play my last card.

—I have a driver's license.

There! Let's sit over there! The parents follow us to a high table in the middle of the restaurant. We toss our coats onto the stools and they fall off, we open the wrappers but mama stops us, wash your hands first. We run toward the last stop between us and bliss, mama manages to snag Nico by the sleeve. There's nothing human about him anymore. His hair is spiky with static from the coat he's just taken off, his cheeks are red, his shoelaces are still dragging and his sweater is on inside out and backwards, the tag glistening with spit. His face is one enormous disgruntlement, he's wild, he's sick of all this. In his eyes the nuggets he's glimpsed are still gleaming. I push on the bathroom door and Nico holds it back with all his might, we yell because our voices echo. Mama holds the door behind us and turns back, sees my father starting in on his fries, the strap of his bag wrapped twice around his wrist.

Nico's already long gone, I rinse my hands and on my way out the door smacks into a potted plant, halfway knocks it over. Behind me mama gets mad as she does so often in public places, unbelievable, can't you be just a little bit careful, bull in a china shop.

—I'd say my biggest weakness is I don't have enough experience.

—Hang on, hang on. That's not a weakness, everybody has to start somewhere, and we train you here. A weakness, give me a weakness, anything, just pick one. Are you impulsive? Do you have a temper?

—No, no.

—You're not scared of Covid, or some other disease?

—No more likely to catch it here than anywhere else.

7

—Good answer. Are you the dreamy type, you tend to forget things?

—No, I mean not really.

—You're not put off by certain chores? Would you mind taking out the trash?

—I do that every week at home.

—Some people think it's disgusting.

—Not me.

—I'd understand if you did.

—Well, if I really think about it … No, that's not a problem for me.

—So you don't have any weaknesses, that's what you're saying? So you're perfect, like me?

When we get back to him my father has already finished all his fries and mama notices, are you kidding me, hey watch out Nico, sleeve in the sauce. The straws are stuck through the center of the transparent lids, the Coke comes up and tickles our throats. My father starts in on his burger, don't drink all the Coke, kiddos, you'll spoil your appetite. Mama divides the sauces between the boxes, gets ketchup on her fingers. Nico starts to put the toy together, she stops him, you can play when you're done eating. I keep quiet. A nugget on my tongue, I feel the breading fall apart, the sauce slip off and dissolve. Our hair shines under the ceiling lights, we have halos.

—Well, I won't lie to you, I have a hundred applications on my desk, not to mention online, I haven't even looked at those yet, and today I still have five more interviews after you.

The boss is about to ask what sets me apart, why should we take you over somebody else. It's not enough to have a car, to live five minutes away, and to be staying on longer than the other applicants. You've also got to want the others to fail their interviews, you've got to want to take the job away from them.

I try to come up with a synonym for adaptable and I can't find one. I can't very well say multifunctional.

So, happy? The four of us are squeezed in around the table and every five minutes my father repeats, so, happy? We're concentrating, do not disturb. The table is sticky, fingerprints, mayonnaise on the rim of the tray. Mama collects the detritus as we push the carcasses aside. My father's telling a story, my first time at a fast-food place, this was back when I was still in technical school, we sucked pieces of ice up our straws and then blew out, sending them sliding down the aisles, good times. He replays his whole life, the orange walls of his kindergarten, detentions in junior high, his technical certification, clattering down the residence-hall stairs in Hérouville to call his parents from a phone booth, yelling into the receiver I want to come home, I can't take it here. His mother is an hour away, tries to reassure him. Calm down now Jérôme, what are you talking about, no you're not going to die, you'll get your degree and then you'll find some little job not too far from home, that's all.

Nico and I gasp in dismay when it's all gone. We look in the bag for the stray fry, the nugget breading we try to pick up with a moist fingertip. So, happy?

—Okay, I've put down mid-September, but can I say late? Would that work for you, to stay on till the end?
—Yes, yes why not?
—Perfect. Of course you can tell me that and then quit whenever you like, right?

All right, we can't hang around, it's getting late and we've still got a long drive. We pretend not to hear, and Nico turns the alien's nose. Lights flash, it's got batteries in it. I'm dumbstruck for a moment, my lips part, and in my mind I see a parade of all my birthday gifts, all my Christmas presents. Waiting to

9

use the creepy hand, the talking teddy bear, the crying baby, the walkie-talkies, the watch. Waiting for my father to go out for batteries.

When will we come back? Mama puts on her coat and my father slips his bag over his shoulder, the strap across his chest. When will we come back? The parents look away. Nico protests that he never went on the slide, that he didn't get a balloon, it's not fair. I'm ready to go, the Velcro on my coat is clawing at my chin, I look at the people who'll be here after we're gone. The ladies in caps are busy behind the counter, their foreheads glowing under the low lamps. Dreaming, I turn the alien's nose but my father stops me, you're going to run down the batteries, you've got to conserve. Nico is crying, mama tugs him by the sleeve. That's the last time we're coming here if it's just going to cause such a fuss! Hardly seems worth it!

I write down my scheduling preferences on a sheet of paper. The interview is over. I hurry toward the exit but just when I reach the automatic doors the boss calls out to me. I see him trotting toward me, you took my pen—watch out that's a very serious infraction here. He's joking. I open my damp palm like I'm swearing an oath and he recovers the pen, tucks it into his shirt pocket. Leaving the restaurant, I know I've got the job.

Because it costs money, that's why we don't go there! You knew we can't stay all night! Nico sniffles into the sleeve of his sweater. I don't dare turn the alien's nose because I know my father would see me in the rearview mirror. He puts the key in the ignition and adds besides, I've got work tomorrow! Vacation's over, we're going home.

I clasp the toy as if it were evidence, proof that this really happened, and then I concentrate because I don't want to hear him say you've got to conserve again. That's all I can think about as the car passes the city limits sign and disappears into the countryside past the streetlights.

✳ ✳ ✳ ✳

—You're late once you get a pass, you're late twice you're out.

The boss waits a beat, looks up from his papers, we hurry to vigorously agree. A friendly chuckle, he adds we understand each other, right, because I know plenty of folks who want a job, so anyone who shows up late that's it, I've got no time for them. He puts a tablet down in front of us, we're supposed to sign with one finger on the lower left. We're sitting on a bench in the middle of the locker room, at the far end a girl in a white shirt is eating a hamburger and looking at her phone. She's got a few minutes before she goes back out.

Someone pushes open the swing door, others come in at the same time, okay if you're scheduled for 11:30 clock-in now, there's a rush on! They say hello to the boss. The door swings, it's painted a mean red, makes you tired just looking at it, they're going to get dressed, a real parade. Girls tie back their hair, put on hairnets, go out again, we see someone pulling on a pair of pants, so long! The door swings the other way, a girl is smoothing down her collar next to my contract and puts the shirt on as soon as it's straight, another is dusting off her pants. Where are you today? Drive-thru drinks desserts, I'm on fries I can't stand it anymore, come on it's not that bad would you rather be with me out front? The girls' faces turn into the faces of Persian cats as they put their hair into ponytails, imprison it in nets. Anybody seen the schedule grid? The door closes again. Silently, we sign our names at the bottom of the contracts.

We're still sitting on the bench, the boss is training us, we train you here, so every half hour you've got to soak the dishcloths in this solution to disinfect them. You have to take the pot, fill it up, pour in this packet, close it up, keep it such and such a distance from the ground, this here's the clean zone, that's the dirty zone. So, little pop quiz to see how much you've understood, what temperature, what distance, how often, when where and why? okay? Right, here we go.

He hands us our plastic-wrapped uniforms, many times dirtied by crew members before us. I don't have a cap. The girl who'd been eating next to us has left without our seeing her stand up, and now we're supposed to follow the boss so he can give us the tour.

He points out the sink on our left, a few tomatoes are lying on the floor, a crew member is spraying off others in stainless steel trays. The drain is under his feet. Boiler room to the right, this is where we keep cleaning supplies. A stack of trash cans hides a doorway, the boss tells us it leads outside, we believe him. We go down the hallway, push open a door. The boss shows us the supply room, there are boxes stacked on shelves. Two wide doors open onto a fridge, the *posi*, and a freezer, the *nég*. A crew member goes in but all we can see is her topknot, the rest is bundled up in an enormous coat with the chain's logo on it. You can't go into the *nég* wearing a crew member's shirt. As we move on, the boss dispels rumors, we don't use soda powders, see these syrup pouches, we get everything straight from Coca-Cola.

We wander among the shelves until we reach a door, the managers' office. You have to knock before you go in. A few paper-strewn desks, and above them surveillance screens follow what's going on in the kitchen, at the counter, and out front. The boss looks around the room, summarizes, this is where the managers do the books and the HR person draws up your schedules. He opens one more door and we end up at the big punch clock, in the middle of the kitchen. It shows the time, you scan your card, press in or out, the clock says hello when you're coming in and nothing when you're going out. Whenever you scan your card the clock makes a noise like a camera flash. That's the end of the tour, the boss leaves us with a trainer. She'll teach us about drive-thru orders and taking payments. Cars are going by on the other side of the glass.

—I can drive if you like.
—No, no, it's fine.

Mama's holding the guide to the best bargain restaurants, my father's at the wheel. We're driving around Quiberon trying to find free parking, it's ten past noon, and after we've circled the town a couple of times my father turns off the radio. At that point the drive goes from sightseeing to a hunt for the restaurant. In the back seat, we've got to keep quiet, let the parents decide, otherwise we'll hear them say all right then we'll go to the supermarket and get ham and bread since you're never happy with anything. For the past few minutes Nico has been muttering that he wants fast food like last year, it's easy, it's close by, there's one there, and there, and over there too, they're all over.

—There, there it is! Mama points at a restaurant we drive past without stopping, ranked one piggy bank out of five. My father parks down the street, and by the door-side menu they talk prices, entrees, three-course prix fixes, yeah but I don't like vinaigrette, so you don't order a first course, I can't skip a course in a prix fixe, or maybe eggs mimosa, I hope they have fries, of course they'll have fries, they have steak. What about you? What looks good?

I'm wearing a headset, the trainer says that's lane two up top, down below is lane one, you push this to talk, when it's red the customer can hear you, if it's blinking there's a car waiting. In the earphone a chime cuts through the words, I want a wrap, I want applesauce, no, no toy, is a toy mandatory in a kid's meal? The trainer's one year older than us, she keeps saying it's actually very simple, it becomes automatic, in the end you get used to it. All you have to do is say hello, thank you, goodbye, say ready to take your order, and if you have to, could you please repeat that, I didn't hear.

The problem with working the drive-thru is the screen I'm facing, where I'm supposed to enter the order. Rectangular boxes, you have to push with your index finger, what do I click on, where are the desserts, how do I leave off an ingredient, add a sauce, a free one, don't charge for sauce, and why do they always want a croque monsieur with no ham? I'm hunched over the screen, my finger goes back and forth in the air whenever someone says something in my earpiece. I want a burger in a combo meal. My finger moves, but where is it, I've lost the burger and I don't know how to cancel the ice cubes, replace the ice cream with a different ice cream and no syrup. The kid in the car tells his mother, uh no not diet Coke, regular Coke, and I have to start over. A customer shows up with a coupon, he cut it from a receipt, can you wait just one moment please? I need a manager's magnetic card to apply the discount. I'll also use that card to open the cash register in case of a mistake and for my meal too, at the end of the shift, that's the *carte mana*, the manager card.

In the beginning I don't know which ones are the manas, everyone sends me to somebody else, ask Antoine, try Caro, ask Laura, and you've got to find them without knowing what they look like, they could be anybody. Everyone has the same uniform, or almost, the managers are the ones who sometimes wear a black pullover or a pair of jeans with pockets, the ones whose clothes change with the seasons. But right now it's summertime and everyone's wearing white shirts. I hand the headset to the trainer and go to the window to learn how to take payments. A truck stops in front of me, a young woman cranks down the driver's-side window. You take holiday vouchers?

Stay outside, we'll ask. Nico kicks at the retaining wall, chanting drive-in, drive-in, and I watch my parents through the restaurant window. I see my father's mouth forming the usual words, his hands squeezing his shoulder bag in the usual way. When he gets his vouchers, they sit there on the table for a couple of weeks, can you imagine that's four hundred and fifty euros in there, and we read the terms and conditions as we eat, four hundred and fifty euros and look we can go all over the place! Nico answers yeah even the drive-in.

The drawer of the cash register pokes me in the stomach, the same register I used to have as a toy, but it gives me a start every time, I'm never expecting it.

My parents come out of the restaurant, the car doors slam and we're off again. The radio is still silent, my father turns the steering wheel more roughly, takes curves at a dangerous speed. Mama goes on giving directions until she cries out right there, there it is, right, well you missed it, it was the turn before, and then my father explodes. His face clenches, his hands grow huge on the wheel, for fuck's sake! And Nico silently kisses his wishes goodbye. My father says give me the map, give me the map I can figure this out better than you. And mama, but you're driving, I mean it doesn't matter, we'll get there. And him, you're a pain in the ass, you're all a pain in the ass, fuck. I look through the window at the industrial zone around us, my father turns into a factory parking lot to turn around, damn it! and mama doesn't say anything more, she lays her hand on the door handle. The buildings go by and the car comes back to the address in the book, do you see a restaurant around here? Kids if you see a restaurant shout out. We both look in different directions, like at the supermarket, and mama softly says I swear this is the address, it's in the guide! All we see are truck factories, tractor factories, and then other ones we can't identify, white warehouses with windows too high up to see through.

—I'd like a bacon.
    —I'm sorry I didn't quite hear you, can you repeat that?
    —A bacon thing, you know, I'm not sure what you call it, bacon something.
    —I'm sorry, could you say that again?

15

—I said a bacon.

—I beg your pardon, I'm new here and I don't know everything, I'm pretty sure we don't have any burgers with just bacon, what is it exactly you want?

—Listen, you're the one who works here honey, you know the sandwiches better than I do.

There, the restaurant, the creperie! My father turns but drives right past the restaurant decorated with scallop shells. His eyes blazing, he speeds back to the campground. Nico takes care not to make eye contact, silence settles in, I take out a book. It's a quarter to one and my father doesn't turn on the radio, doesn't stop at the supermarket. Mama closes her guide to the best restaurants, pulls her sweater up over her face and goes to sleep.

—Give her to me, I'll talk to her.

—It's my fault, I didn't understand what she wanted.

—Give her to me. Madame? Are you still there?

✳ ✳ ✳ ✳

I punch in the code, chime, I open the door. The women's locker room is a long rectangle split by a row of orange lockers and a sink. There's someone sitting on the one chair, I put on my pants behind the swing door. This is my second day. On the door, I read that we're not supposed to leave our clothes in the locker room when we're not working and we're supposed to take off our earrings. The lockers have labels, the names of the women who work here or worked here long ago, still remembered for their longevity, one set a record, almost seven years, and revered for the day when, shit, she poked a hole through the bottom of the ice cream bucket, when she spilled a whole bag of caramel sauce on her pants, when she insulted a customer, she was really something.

The new girls have to prove themselves before they get their name on a locker door. You can tell who's been around a while by their slightly faded labels. I'm assigned the locker used to store work pants.

Soon it will be noon, clouds of deodorant, hairnets on the floor. The tiles are wet from morning to night, the damp never goes away. Some of the girls go out to the entryway where they iron their shirts. They say, you're new here right, how long have you been here, and soon they move on to when do you get off today, what are your weekend days? The crew members shake out their white shirts and put on their shoe covers. The introductions have been made.

It might be afternoon, another year. Nico walks down a white gravel path, following the signs, he turns right, left, locates the toilets, takes a few steps, okay, this is it. I follow him, two pillows under my arms, and I watch my shoes turning white. I want to take them off and throw them far away, get to the grass and rub my dusty toes through it, but Nico walks faster than I do, I'm running on tiptoe. We end up at a sandy patch, two swing sets with fraying ropes, the merry-go-round that makes you throw up, horses on springs, burning hot slide, its underside rusty. Nico digs in the sand and I stand up on a swing. My father is paying at the entrance, mama's with him, we're waiting to find out our campsite number. Beyond the play area there are rows of tents, some have a table in front of them, shoes outside, bicycles with the rental number on the frame, stoves leaned against the tent stakes to cool off. Darkness is already falling behind the pines. Clotheslines are hung from a chain-link fence, bashed in as if somebody tried to climb it one night, tried again, then gave up.

Our tent has three rooms, one for the parents, one for Nico, one for me. I already know I'll put my sleeping bag at the back, my piled-up clothes to the left and my books, notebooks, and pencils on the right. I'm already thinking about the crow that

17

will start cawing at six o'clock, and then the cooing pigeon, and the warm sleeping bag, zipped all the way up at night and thrown off in the morning, the sound of the tent zipper, the one that sometimes means that's enough now it's time to sleep, the mosquito net you zip up behind you, the flashlights recharging, Nico's snoring just a few seconds after he zips up his mosquito net, the movie my father's watching, the mattress you have to pump up every morning and every night, I did put some tape on it last year, there's a hole somewhere but I can't find it, here stand on it so I can look for it. All that will happen, but for the moment the tent's still in the trunk and Nico is holding his stomach, he's jumped off the merry-go-round.

—Anybody have the time? Who's lunch mana today?

Children we don't know come along, a little better dressed than us. Nico's lying flat on his stomach in the sand, breathing gently so he won't throw up, and I'm still perched on the swing so I won't die. Our clothes are rumpled, wrong for the weather, our fingers are greasy, our scalps itch. We look away, me above and Nico below, even if I suspect he's faking it, I don't come down. We ignore the other children, we're not here. Better to meet them tomorrow. Nico sits up, takes off one shoe and shakes it. The children ride the merry-go-round and don't vomit. I try to decide what activities I'll choose for the week—day at the zoo, treetop adventure, beach. The children examine us as if we weren't invisible, then they clap their hands and laugh loudly. The little girl has green sandals. Mama comes into the play area, strides over and squats down close by us. She tells us the site number like every year, but this time she adds be nice to your father this week, he's completely worn out. Mama's pant cuffs are dirty. Nico plucks a dandelion, puts on a peevish air, asks why? She briefly closes her eyes, see that's what I mean, I don't want you bugging him with your questions, he's exhausted from all the driving, he needs a little break from home, from work.

Mama stands up. The cooler slung over her shoulder makes her limp across the gravel to the front office. Nico lies down again, he gags, he's breathing with his vocal cords, I say you okay? you okay Nico? The little girl claps a musical toy to her ear, she sings *No no no no don't*, I don't care. The pillows fall off the bench where I left them, into the dust, and I get off the swing. Nico springs for my leg, clutches my ankle sock. Tag, I'm it.

—Anyone seen the schedule grid?

—I'll have a blue frosty please madame.

　—Okay, I'm putting some in your cup now.

　—*Glug glug*, thank you madame, it's very good, how much does it cost.

　—It's a hundred.

　—Hey, that's gone up, last time it was ten.

　—Yes, but there's inflation.

　—No, we said there wasn't.

　—There is, everybody knows it and everybody says so. It's a hundred and that's all there is to it.

　—I only have a fifty, let's just say it doesn't matter.

　—You drank the frosty so pay up or I'm calling the police.

　—You have a cell phone?

　—Or I'll yell really loud.

　—I gave you a deal on the fruit last time, but you're never nice to me.

　—That will be a hundred, and if you're not happy it's still the same.

　—But I don't have enough money, can I pay you by patting your hand?

　—...

19

—This is the last time, I promise, next time I'll have enough money.

—Go on, *pat, pat*.

A crew member disinfects the headset he's about to hand me, runs the cloth over the earpiece, wipes the microphone. I put it on like a headband, I move the microphone toward my mouth, ready to enter the orders on the screen in front of me. The trainer's the same as yesterday, unchanged from the day before except that under her hairnet a lock of hair is pinned down differently, it makes a stray curl near her ear. The trainer rubs the corner of her eye, she stands behind me, I push the button for line two.

—Hello! The others usually know me, I don't recognize your voice. I'm the lady who likes oat milk in her morning coffee, could you do that for me? And an extra water please, for my dog.

—Hello I'm ready to take your order, and what else can I get you? would you like me to put the burgers on screen? would you like anything on it? would you like a dessert? would you like anything else? will that be all today? fourteen euros fifty, I'll let you pull ahead to payment, thank you, goodbye hello, fourteen euros fifty, by card? goes here, here's your ticket, delivery lane 1, hello may I take your order.

—Hello one child's meal, girl.

—Yes?

—For a girl.

—What combo would you like?

Jérôme says he can't relax. Even though he left his shoulder bag at home, even though the children are cute, he says that a lot, you're cute, kids, even though Sylvie dealt with the reservations this year. When he takes off his shoes to walk on the sand and unfurls a towel to sit down, he stares at the ocean as if someone were drowning out there and he can't do anything about it. In the amusement park he recognizes the machines, he says they've got that brand at the factory, for riveting car doors. At the campground he struggles endlessly with the irreparable. The beach umbrella stand has a crack, he whistles, goes to the trunk for a toolbox and a roll of duct tape, no one can see what he's talking about, but when he fixes something he always says I'll try holding it together with duct tape. Sometimes Jérôme throws himself down the slide into the campground pool, he cuts his buckwheat crepe into little squares at the restaurant, he chases Nico with a squirt gun. But in the evening he talks about work, he gnaws at his thumbnail, Sylvie says stop it, I can't stand that, and then he gets a nail infection.

When he comes across a cat on a hike, Jérôme takes a half-hour break to scratch the kitty's head, to kneel down and give it a friendly nudge with his brow. Then he puts on his backpack full of bottled water and buckles it in front. He reminds us that they gave it to him at work, he tests all the zippers saying that's quality, except for the broken one in back. At night, in the streets of Crozon, he holds Sylvie's hand and for a moment raises his thumbnail to his mouth but it's bandaged, he drops his hand back to his side.

When Jérôme fixes things he always wounds himself before he succeeds, as if the brokenness had to pass from the object to his body before it can disappear. Sylvie asks him to stop fixing that piece of crap, who cares if it works, we don't need one, we've got four radios already. Sometimes all she says is this isn't going to end well.

Every repair job ends with Jérôme putting on Mercuro-chrome, not even thinking about it. He shows us the fruit of his labors, but all we can see is his punctured hands, the cuts, the bandages, we cover our eyes and Jérôme tells us he's just made us some money, this way we won't have to buy a new one. Sylvie gives up protesting, she asks him to reserve places for the treetop adventure tomorrow, but before he dials the number he gets worried, what do I say? what time do we want? do I have to reserve the equipment too? Once the information has been provided and the number dialed, he turns again to Sylvie.

—What do I say if they ask me something else and I don't know?

✳ ✳ ✳ ✳

—I'm sorry, I'm new here, I was a little slow typing in your order.
—I'll say.
—Forgive me.
—How about a goodwill discount?

The trainer shakes her head and I pull my mike back up, you can pull ahead to the payment window, that will be thirty-seven euros. In the middle of the kitchen the punch clock makes an Italian car horn sound because someone's late punching out and the evening team, the relief crew, is finally coming in. They wait for their start time, they've got their cards out, ready to scan. Some of them watch the seconds go by and others look over the schedule, checking what station they've got for this shift. They crack jokes, they tie on their plastic aprons, I'm in the kitchen, where are you, out front, weren't you there yesterday? The car horn drowns out the rest of their conversation.

Seven o'clock comes and one by one they lay their cards on the scanner, the punch clock says hello seven times. One crew member lays down her card and the time clock starts chattering, minimum break period not taken, it explains. They all go off to their stations in silence, the car horn still honking. I take orders, I forget all the faces that say hello to me. The trainer's standing behind me, mechanically readying the kid's-combo meal boxes. Someone comes over, calls out to the trainer, hey that's you honking, time for you to clock out, did

22

you forget? The trainer wishes me luck before running off to the locker room.

I lost an earring while I was hanging from a cord in the tree-tops. The back came loose and the gold butterfly fell. We spent a long time looking for it under the trees, and I cried to make the earring reappear. I cried to make the person who decides how the story comes out take pity on me, but it didn't work. My father flipped over the dead leaves to be sure it hadn't slipped through, he walked the whole course where my earring had fallen off. Mama was saying don't worry about it Jérôme, we'll buy another one, but this wasn't about money. The sky turned royal blue, the park would be closing any time now, and my father was running along the paths, saying again and again it's not possible, it can't have gone far. The lamps came on, we lost my father, the park guards making their closing rounds sent him back to us. He hadn't found my earring, he came to tell me, head hanging.

Every evening after that I have to close myself away in a wash hut with mama so she can disinfect my ears. The surviving butterfly has to be switched from one ear to the other so the holes won't close up. Mama takes the opportunity to crush a few head lice in the sink, and when she says that's a big one I shake my comb-tousled head in protest, I don't want to hear one word about the colony growing every day around my roots. I see the bugs falling from my wet hair and the blood on the cotton, mama says hold still, she grabs me by the back of the neck. My chin is on the white sink, mama's fingernails go click click, I can hear her pressing the lice and nits to make them burst, tick tick, I close my eyes but that noise goes on, the sound of the lice being flattened against the porcelain.

A dad dumps a bunch of centimes into my cupped hands. On the surveillance screen, a traffic jam. A motorcycle honks, a driver gets out and grabs hold of the motorcyclist. A man walks past with a piece of cardboard that says he's hungry, customers close their windows on his fingers. In my headset, lane two, I hear a woman yelling into a phone for fuck's sake the least you can do is show up for a date, Jonathan! If you can't understand that, shut up shut up shut up, you said that before so just shut up, I don't want to hear it, no you listen to me, because last time, just last time you said, no, but you said you were ready, I can't believe this, just stop! A baby is crying in the back seat. The woman hangs up. I finish counting the change and the dad bends toward me.

—Sorry, that's from the kids' piggy bank.

I come out of the wash hut and pad barefoot over the gravel to the tent, relieved when I finally get to the grass where I can run. My wet hair comes unstuck from my neck and dries as it flops. It's dark out, behind me campers are singing karaoke. A couple has launched into a song for two, a breakup song, but it's nothing serious, this is our chance, for once we're both singing. It's a little cold, and outside the tent I stub my toe on a duct-tape-wrapped tent stake. I stop and don't go in, I sit down cross-legged by the front flap. The couple reaches the chorus again, *tu m'oublieras tu m'oublieras*, applause, a disco song starts up while others pore over the list of tracks they can sing to, dither, make up their minds.

My pajama bottoms stick to my not-yet-dry legs. In the distance, standing stones, the menhirs we came here to see, you can see them beyond the swimming pool and the play area. I hear the movie my father is watching inside the tent on the player he got at Christmas from the workers' council, a man talks, then there are gunshots and cries of pain. At the karaoke machine someone's gone for Edith Piaf, and everyone joins in, *padam padam padam*. The emcee sings louder than rest, he's hung on to a microphone. An invisible bug crawls onto my leg and I crush it, possibly a mosquito. The distant singer is holding a note, *comme si tout mon passé défilait*, applause, but the song isn't over. Behind the clapping the girl with the mike goes on *cet air qui bat*, no one's listening anymore, and the DJ fades into an Indochine song. I scratch at my scalp. Thanking the singer, the emcee reminds the crowd that they'll have a chance to vote for the best.

The gravel crunches under mama's feet, she appears in the nimbus of the battery-powered garden lamp.

—Aren't you coming in?

—It's a little too hot, I won't be long.

—Nico's taking his shower.

—Papa's watching a movie.

—All packed for tomorrow?

—Yes, everything's in.

—Did you leave your swimsuit out?

—Why?

—We'll have one last dip in the pool tomorrow morning before we go.

—No, I didn't leave it out.

—The pool's there waiting, do as you like but you might as well enjoy it.

—Where are we eating tomorrow?

The client grabs the card reader to pay, yanks it toward him, pulling it off its base, the reader falls under the car. I hurry to the front counter for a mana, I say the machine fell under, it came off, two pieces, the customer can only do a card, I don't know how to talk anymore. The crew member before me says I'm not a manager, ask Laura, she's in the posi. When I find her I say some more words, I only know ten or so, the ones I've been using for the past four hours. An hour from now the punch clock will blow its horn and it will be my turn to get out of here.

—I'm sorry?

—The machine fell, he grabbed, he wants to pay, I don't know, should I go around?

—I don't understand a word you're saying.

25

—The machine, it's under the Citroën, and the customer wants to pay.

Laura is a counter manager, twice my circumference. Her glasses are pushed up on top of her head and she's not wearing a hairnet. She keeps her card in her jeans pocket and only takes it out if she's in the mood. When crew members go looking for a mana, they're not looking for Laura. Often her answer is I couldn't care less, deal with it. When Laura walks she puts all her weight on her left leg, and when she's in a hurry everyone stands back, she's frightening, she jostles the cooks as she goes by. Laura never says excuse me.

She heads for my station, breathing loudly as I repeat the Citroën, it's the Citroën at the pay station, it's, it won't, we have to.

I lie on my air mattress and listen to the sound of the highway that runs past the campground, unless it's coming from an airport. I can't say why, but you don't hear it in the daytime. It's not car tires, it's more like a continuous rushing sound, as if all the trucks in the world were working in shifts to create a harmony, the perfect white noise. I know it well, I've heard it before, from my bedroom window.

We moved to this town of two thousand the day my father found a better job. The apartment is as close to unbounded countryside as it is to a heavily traveled road. When my father talks about his last job he says Besnier or Charchigné, he never goes into detail. That's all it takes to name what you have to get away from. We live on the third floor, and every evening when I open the door to my room that constant sound of rolling trucks reminds me I'm in a town that's on the way to someplace else, and that same logic tells me I'll be going away too one day.

✳ ✳ ✳ ✳

—And for dessert?
—Pineapple slices.

—Excuse me?
—Pineapple slices.
—I'm sorry, would you please say that again?
—Pineapple slices!
—I, no, what did you say?
—Pineapple slices!
—Look I'm really sorry, the thing is, I don't know if I can't hear you right, or—
—Pineapple slices!

In the car, the spitty finger has scoured the bottom of the potato-chip bag, over and back, nothing left. Maybe we've all slept too long or maybe the saturated fat has gone to our heads, maybe the radio's too loud but my father's been driving for five hours and the first time we asked he answered in his mad voice, so we don't dare try again. Their batteries drained, the game consoles are lying next to a blue cooler, Nico's mattress, mama's sweater, brochures from the Paimpont tourist office, two pillows, and a box of aniseed candy. Nico and I laugh at the cars behind us, we stick out our tongues at them, we laugh at the cops who've stopped someone at the roundabout, we laugh at him, we laugh at me, and with every laugh we slap each other's legs and knees and Nico is gasping for breath, his face turns red, purple, he can't breathe and his hands open and close like he's trying to catch me, his eyes closed, his chest racked by spasms, and finally he lets out the ringing laugh I know by heart.

Reflected in the fogged-up window, I'm a scarlet monster with a deformed face, my skin creased like failed origami, and I'm spitting, my tongue between my two front teeth, I spit like I'm gargling while I talk. Sweat and saliva mingle on Nico's forehead, his nostrils are flaring. I can see his gapped teeth when he shouts, yellowed by the noontime potato chips and ham-and-butter sandwich. He always shouts before his laugh erupts and explodes against the right-hand back door, the one that never closes right, that we have to open and slam shut again five minutes after the car's started off. This time Nico's shout goes on and on, the parents yell at him but he doesn't stop, the laugh won't come and I grab his fine, blond, damp hair, bury his head in one of the pillows like I was trying to suffocate him, then I pull him up and do it again, time after time I spare his life and then the laugh comes, deep in the pillow, with a long string of spit. When I let go of his head a few hairs, almost white they're so shiny, stay wrapped around my fingers and Nico looks at me with his mouth turned down.

—Pineapple slices!
    —I've got static in my headset, something's crackling, I don't know what to say to you. We have ice cream, in a cup or on a cone, and fruit, what would you like?
    —Pineapple slices!

Hand in hand we shove and claw, and under the red it's white, we slap and slap and slap, our cheeks are on fire, and then our hands lash out at random, anywhere, legs, arms, we don't even look where we're slapping anymore, all that matters is to feel we got in a good smack somewhere. Our hands clench, fists pummel stomachs, noses, and that's when my father stops us, look there it is! We drive past the factory, we make out the car-part maker's logo on the front. My father honks once and two men in the back of the sheet-metal hangar raise their arms. My father expounds, those trash cans on the side over there, that's where I find stuff to take home, we're not really supposed to but what can you do, you've got to get something out of working there. Mama's looking the other way, toward the forest that spreads out further on. Once we're past the factory Nico leans back. He stretches out diagonally on the inflatable mattress, kicks at me, his tennis shoes batter my head and I take up the same position, my shoes in his face, bam bam bam and finally Nico's nose explodes, the blood flows, fills his mouth, runs down his chin. Nico bursts out laughing and blood spatters my face, reddens the dust on his shoes. Vacation's over, my father is relieved, and he starts to sing shrilly over a guitar solo.

—So you want fruit, fine, that much I understand. We have sliced apples, we have mango.
    —Pineapple slices!
    —But monsieur, we don't sell that!
    —Oh, okay.
Ten o'clock, end of the rush, all the work stations are slowing down. I leave the drive-thru booth and walk through the kitchen. The crew member on fries is still hard at it even as everyone else is relaxing, she's hung a basket on the metal rim of the fryer and she pours in a bagful of frozen fries, half of them land on the floor where they'll be crushed under our shoe covers. I pick up a broom so no one will yell at me for not sweeping the floor and I walk past two managers leaning over the counter. They're sorting the different-colored cardboard boxes as they come out from the kitchens. Someone pours out a bucket of water to scrub the caramel off the floor, somebody else is wrapping containers in plastic wrap. On the surveillance screen above the fries, I see a car at my drive-thru and hurry back to my station.

I'm taking payment from the customer who wants four ice creams in the middle of the night when I realize there's water lapping around my feet. I've been clocked in for hours and never noticed the half inch of water menacing my work pants. I drape my headset over my neck and blankly set out upstream in search of the source. The leak is coming from the drive-thru hall, a sort of tube where crew members open windows, run back and forth, and store boxes of sauce. The water makes lopsided puddles in invisible low spots, the tiles seem hollowed out where the crew members shuffle in place. I go on, my legs carry me forward all on their own. Like a child happily walking through water in her boots, I wade without

29

danger in my shoe covers. My earpiece shrills, there's a car waiting. I go back, splash around at my station, put the headset back on. A car is parked at my window, and in the back seat I can only see the hair of a child slumped against the window.

With every jolt of the Berlingo my head bounces against the glass, my right cheek is almost stuck to it. I don't try to sleep. Mama's face has disappeared under a sweater, all you can see is her half-open mouth. Whenever I scratch my head I tell myself this is the last time, I'll give it a good hard scratch and that will be it. In the door, Kleenex, CDs, and a hairbrush tied up in butcher's twine. I jam my feet against the window. Nico has turned off his game console, he's snoring on his pillow. When it comes time to get out, in front of the house, I know he'll pretend to be sleeping so the parents will carry him in to bed. The garage light will shine on his solemn face and my father will bend over him, he's giggling, he's not really asleep look he's giggling. Nico will clench his lips, knit his brow, fake a soft snore. There's only one way to know if he really is sleeping. A tickle under the arms and Nico won't be able to hold back, he'll start kicking in every direction, knowing perfectly well he can give up on being carried in now. Sometimes Nico will be so sound asleep that the parents don't dare carry him for fear of waking him up, they'll leave him in the car, unlocked in case he comes to, the garage light still on. I've stopped wanting to be carried. Last time mama carried me she put me down when we got to the staircase, she said my back hurts, it's because of work. The scotch tape on one arm of her glasses spoke of her most recent tussle with one of the teenagers at the center. Every time school started up in the fall I never knew how to explain what sort of work she did.

In the rearview mirror, I study my father's face, tragic, invested with the mission of getting us home again. He glances back to see if we're asleep and I close my eyes as hard as I can so he'll think so. Mama wakes up.

—Be careful, okay?

—Don't worry I've slowed down.

—I mean about work, I don't want them putting you back in that post.

—I've told them about that, but what more do you want me to do.

—You can't keep going up in the cherry picker with nobody on the ground.

—It's been reported, but they couldn't care less, you know how it is.

My father pushes the big button on the radio and I half open my eyes. The illuminated dial tells the time. The car bounces over a speed bump, and when we reach Christ on the cross my father flips the turn signal.

— Be careful, okay?

— Don't worry, I've slowed down.

— I mean about work. I don't want them putting you back in that pit.

— I've told them about that, but what more do you want me to do.

— You can't keep [illegible] with nobody on the ground.

— It's been reported, but they couldn't care less, you know how it is.

My father pushes the big button on the radio and I hold open my eyes. The illuminated dial [illegible] the tunnel. The car bounces over a speed bump, and when we reach [illegible] on the [illegible] my father flips the turn signal.

OUT FRONT

This one's my all-time fave, it smells so nice. The front-room trainer holds the special-surfaces cleaner under her nose. I love it, I just can't get enough, want a sniff?

She juggles the cleaning products this way and that, pretends to spray a surface to show us how, but as she demonstrates all I can see is the tight blonde bun behind her head, as if her brain had an annex back there.

The trainer introduces us to the sink, the clean zone. This is where it all starts, she explains, and we trample the stray bits of food on the floor drain. Before sending us out front she takes us into the bathroom to teach us by example, pulls out a disinfectant for the sinks. She rubs at the sink with a counter cloth, that's what it's called, presses her breasts to the rim to get behind the faucets. Not one single hair sticks out of her bun, it seems to have a life of its own, independent of her movements no matter how vigorously she scours the surface.

She caresses the soap dispenser and explains that we also have to wipe off the bathroom door handle. She dribbles a purple fluid over the top of a steel trash can and I find my head spinning. There are too many different fruits in all those scents and I'm fixated on that blonde bun's imperviousness to her body's back-and-forths. I lean on the tall trash can, about to faint, and she tosses the cloth aside, straightens up to take out the phone in her back jeans pocket. I reflexively put my hand to the backside of my pants but my fingers find only a seam, a ridge of fabric folded over itself. As for my shirt pocket, it's scarcely big enough for three packets of ketchup.

Once she's checked her phone the trainer picks up the pace: order kiosks, cleaner, cloth every thirty minutes, wash your hands and change the garbage bag, one-way signs on the tables, running with two trays, hands in crab position, just like a little crab you see, knot the garbage bag and then the compactor, high chairs, stickers, sauces are at the counter, keep an eye out and take the trays to the tables as soon as they're ready, one of you at the greeter station, one out front, standing broom.

Three weeks on drive-thru and now out front, the king-dom nobody wants, composed of the inner lobby where the customers eat, the terrace, the bathroom, and the trash room. I'm out front because I'm new here and the newbie's place is where nobody ever wants to work. I understand I'm going to be here for a while. When I pick up a tray to take out to a table I know the crew members behind the counter had to fight for their cushy spot, shielded by that rectangle of concrete.

I learn that the trainer's name is Chouchou and she's the manager out front. Chouchou goes on to say that everyone loves her here, and when she walks through the automatic door at noon she turns around and calls out see you girls, so happy to have the break ahead of her.

The key turns in the lock and we look up from our homework. Mama smiles, the back-to-school poems don't matter now, she whispers, amused, it's daddy, daddy's home. Nico pushes back his chair and leaps into the arms of the man stopped on the doormat smelling of hair gel and saying hang on, hang on, I have to take off my jacket. When it's my turn to cling to his neck he protests again, no no don't touch me I'm a mess. My father comes home at one in the afternoon when he's on the morning shift, nine at night when he's on the afternoon, five in the morning when he's on the night shift. We always forget the schedule, we're never expecting him and we're always surprised to hear the key turning. When he's not home we know he's at work, and when he comes home we know he'll be leaving again but we don't know when. Yes you do, mama tells us again and again, he's on morning, he's on afternoon, he's on night, but none of that means anything.

He takes off his black leather coat and goes off to wash his hands in the kitchen. Only then does he take off his safety shoes and head for his place on the couch, where the foam has made a hollow for him. He picks up the remote, turns to the news channels, and we put away our notebooks, mama sets a glass dish down in the middle of the table, we lay out the plates. When everything's ready my father turns off the TV, sits down, starts to tell us about his day. The dirty wipes he and his coworkers threw at each other, the funny changes he made to the little handwritten want ads tacked up on the cork bulletin board, the coworkers saying you're a dope Jéjé you're a dope. Mama serves second helpings of quiche. My father tells us about the early-morning rabbits in the factory parking lot, a coworker tried to catch one with a shrimp net but no luck, they're too fast, though somebody found one dead by the side of the road, he put it in a computer tower for a joke, we'll see how long it stays there with the smell. My father holds out his glass for more water. Time to reserve for the workers' council fishing trip, we got the Christmas catalogs, they come at the start of the school year these days so everyone has plenty of time to look through them. Also have to see about tickets for circus day and the boss's farewell party, that's in two weeks. Nico puts his elbows on either side of his plate, when I grow up I want to do what daddy does, and mama asks who wants another piece, come on you're not going to leave me with this, there's almost nothing left, I'm not putting that in the fridge, come on somebody help out, Nico, come on, I'm not just going to stand here holding this dish. My father gets up to turn out the light and go back to his spot on the couch, he peels an orange while the TV casts a blue light on his face. We

35

clear the table in the dark. My father's mouth is shut tight, no more funny stories to tell, he's told them all. My father pries apart the orange segments with his knife.

Chouchou's back, she had a nice lunch, she asks what did you manage to get done while I was away? There are three of us out front and she assigns us tasks because otherwise we wouldn't know what to do with ourselves. Chouchou wonders how we'd ever get along without her. She pulls on a sweater when she gets cold and fingers her big phone when she goes out for a smoke break. I can't leave till 4:30, I press the button on the card reader to check the time.

Chouchou worries I'll get bored so she suggests things for me to do, once around with the standing broom, change the counter garbage bags, she asks if it would be too much trouble to clean the bathroom. Before I can start off she turns toward another crew member and says to her unbelievable, everybody knows how to do that, so why don't you? If I ever evaluate you I'm not even going to give you average, changing a garbage bag in the middle of a rush, what kind of sense does that make? Not knowing my name, she can't call me out, and when she's overwhelmed, when a kid has spilled a drink, she calls me Missy.

Chouchou puts on an apron from the café space and claims she's deep in another task. She takes a customer's money and complains to a crew member, that's two minutes he was waiting and then I had to deal with it, simply not acceptable, when there's somebody waiting you take his money right away. Chouchou says I want you to go once around the …, I sent out what's her name to the tables, you do the bathroom, you do the tables, you do the woodwork with a little cloth. We're working in Chouchou's sitting room.

Once my father has finished the orange and the chocolate bar and eaten all his fingernails he turns off the TV and heads for his room. Mama joins him, the door closes, we can't hear,

36

they're talking, they seem to be taking stock of the day. Some-times the voices rise, as if they'd forgotten how thin the walls are, then fall back into a secret murmur.

I generally make use of that time to pick up my things from all over the apartment. I assemble my books, my games, my rubber bands, my test sheets on the dining room table, between the butter and the butcher's twine. In the front hall I pick up my shoes from next to my father's and wonder if I should leave them there by the door, since that's where they belong. But if I don't gather up everything, if one single belonging escapes this procedure, how can I see the inventory through to the end? The shoe question comes up again and again, every single time.

I measure the passage of time as I walk through the apart-ment. The world map tacked to the bathroom wall is wrinkling. While we were waiting for Santa Claus we tore off pieces of wallpaper behind the living room couch, and on the gray carpet of my parents' bedroom my spilled nail-polish stain now has a permanent crust. My father didn't make his mad face that day. It was the day Nico dropped the plasma globe, and smashed it on the dining room floor, that he got really angry.

Bored? Now you can do the exteriors, and what do I mean by the exteriors? So, you see the terrace, the parking spots over there? You see the black car near the exit? You see the drive-thru, the entrance, the embankments with grass and palm trees? That's what I mean. Walk around with your garbage bag and your broom, pick up the cups, the bags, the paper napkins, the hamburger wrappers, the sauce packets, the straws the spoons the ice cream dishes, the tissues the receipts the cigarette butts the gum.

I end up putting my shoes back in the front hall a few days later. Outside my room the junk is climbing the walls, the furniture's too big for the apartment and my father always says I can't believe this, it's hereditary, it's in the genes. I put my shoes back but to my relief I've brought together all my coats, my bracelets, my test papers, I'm not overrun by stuff. By putting my things together I break the heredity chain like Nico broke the plasma globe that rainy day. I never forget to close the door to my room.

✳ ✳ ✳ ✳

The invasion began in the prehensile thumb. First it went white under the effect of the noninvasive medical hardware disinfectant we use to clean trays, and then my hand was adorned with a very distinctive callus, a callus pumiced, soaked, and massaged with creams, but which will never go away. Every day Chouchou puts me at the greeter station, where trays and table number markers are stacked, and I start my shift without a glance at the assignment chart. Chouchou's never going to let me go. I head straight from the locker room to the sink to pick up my cloth: I know I'm out front today.

Every front-room crew member has a white thumb, it's a fact, their skin flakes and sloughs off when they wash their hands. I ask for gloves but they're not allowed during Covid, you clean a dirty surface with your gloves on and then you touch a customer tray with those gloves, forget it. Covered by the counter cloth for five hours, covered by the damp rag that cleans tables, trays, table number markers, and kiosks, your hand seems just fine. Only in the morning, by the light of the sun, do you see the skin peeling, rub your palm with your fingers and they flake. Before long it's noon. The door opens and closes, a crew member is pulling on her pants, her tennis shoes already hidden by shoe covers and anybody seen the grid? On a countertop in the kitchen our names are written in boxes by a manager, that's the grid, a map of the restaurant with our misspelled first names. Only the privileged few still hope, standing before the schedule grid, for a better station than yesterday's. If you're new here you know perfectly well where you'll be put.

Chouchou is untouched by the invasion. Her thumbs are pristine and when I show her mine flaking away she goes off for her cigarette break. The very tips of her nails are coated with white polish, matching her phone case. She must dust the polish with sparkles before it dries when she puts it on in the evening.

—Who'd you invite over?
—I didn't invite anyone over, mama. The thing is I walked home, there were some other girls walking with me and I asked if they wanted to come in but they didn't stay long.
—Without our permission?
—How could I?
—Call us at work. You have our numbers.
—But it was just a quick little thing, and besides I didn't plan it in advance.
—So you invite people into our house without asking us and that's not a problem.
—I didn't really invite them, since they didn't stay.
—What do you think I am, stupid?
—No, I swear, they looked at my posters and then they went away.
—Jérôme, you hear what your daughter's saying?
—I was just showing them my room.
—Was it clean at least?
—Yes, I mean I think it was, anyway they didn't see the rest.
—They didn't see the rest?
—They didn't see the rest, they came through the dining room, I showed them my room, and then they left.
—So they did see the rest.
—Just barely, and besides they don't care.
—Jérôme, you hear this? Don't you have anything to say?
—I won't do it again, I didn't think it would be a problem.
—Oh, is that so? Suppose we showed people your room when you're not around, suppose we showed them your room in a mess, before you could straighten it?

39

—But in this case everything was all right, it wasn't a mess, everything was just like it usually is.

—Jérôme!

—Besides, they're two good friends of mine.

—Which changes what? You do not invite people in when we're not here, is that clear?

—There wasn't anything wrong and besides I really don't think they care. They said they liked my posters, and then they went away.

—I don't want to hear it! Damn it we can't trust you anymore, we trust you with the keys and you bring your girlfriends in. What's next?

—Nothing's next, they were only just dropping by!

—You're damn right nothing's next. We're still in charge here! You can have over anyone you like when you've got an apartment but until then that's how it is. Ask your father!

Jérôme holds up one index finger next to his ear.

—Listen.

—To what?

—Shh, listen. Don't you hear it?

—Hear what?

—The downstairs neighbors' parrot.

—Oh yeah? What, is he whistling?

—No, listen, he's not whistling.

—What the?

—It's fucking hilarious.

—What?

—Listen ... he's going to say it again.

—What?

—Sarkozy sucks.

I've brought out all the sauces, I've met all the requests, have you done the garbage bags? I've done all the garbage bags, I've turned off the automatic door so I could clean it and I've used the little cloth for the woodwork, I've cleaned the bathroom several times, the order kiosks, the floor. All the tables have been cleared, I've gathered up all the trays and then disinfected them.

Time stretches out after two o'clock. The dining room's no longer a sanctum to be defended against external attacks, now it's just a place you hate. The order kiosks by the entrance, the already ransacked balloon tree, the tables cleaned hundreds of times, the aisles you've walked in every possible direction, the three trash cans. The entrance to the outside playground is closed off by red and white tape. I don't even want to go outside anymore, the terrace disgusts me and wasps lay eggs in the trash cans.

My coworkers are wondering what they'll eat after their shift. They imagine what they're going to whip up and their fingers wriggle gently, they already know where they'll be touching the order screen. Their thumbs are still coated with cleaner, mine are dry and already starting to flake. Nothing's going on in the dining room, but you always have to keep moving, find something, scrub the feet of the drinks machine with a toothbrush, clean the screens in the kitchen, make up salads, but Chouchou's already at that in an apron. If we beat her to something, she stands behind us and criticizes us for filling the boxes too full, then grabs the tongs to show us. Then she takes over the station, says go see out front, they need you, but out front there's nothing to do.

I look at the time on the payment kiosk, five minutes have gone by, some of my coworkers are already clocking out. Chouchou says good thing you're here, otherwise there wouldn't be anyone left out front. I look at her sparkly fingers, she smells like cigarettes. She adds, I got you put out front because you know what you're doing.

After school, I sit upside down on the couch. I drape my legs over the back and my head holds up my body, my face turns purple, and Nico's does faster than mine when he joins me.

The ceiling becomes the floor and the clutter a minor detail, an inventive ceiling light. The floor is white, a bulb sits enthroned in the center of the room but everything's gone, the rooms are bigger, I can run all the way round them, I don't have to worry about seeing my things buried under the clutter, under the shoeboxes, the clothes waiting to be ironed. I have to dig through the pile to find a T-shirt, a notebook, a homework assignment. Stuff piles up in that tiny apartment and I can never find what I'm looking for. My father brought us home, he said he was on morning and once we got there he settled down in the middle of the clutter without moving anything because it's hereditary. In the foam's hollow, he takes off his shoes and then Nico runs off for a spray bottle and fifteen different combs and we sit down above him, on the back of the couch. We start by parting my father's hair down the middle.

At three o'clock Chouchou steps away from the salads, takes a walk around and exclaims why this dining room is impeccable. She congratulates the room and asks what I got up to while she wasn't giving me jobs, I tell her and she goes straight off to smoke her cigarette. Between three and four, my main activity is trying to take over the counter crew members' stations as they clock out, in hopes I can stay there as long as possible. I'm trying to cross over to the other side, but after a few minutes I'm replaced by the incoming shift. I envy the crew member who prints the order ticket and clips it to the tray, which means it's ready to be taken out front. With that task behind her the crew member looks up and I stare at her. Let me just finish disinfecting a table number and then off I go, I just have to put down what I've got in my hands to serve, I tell her that with my eyes, yes I'm coming, I've seen the whole thing, I saw you adding the sauces, the napkins, I know the order's complete and besides that's all I've got to do, serve, I'm available, I'm capable of taking that initiative. The crew member calls for me all the same, she's looking right at me and she calls for me.

My father's hair is plastered down, like we'd smeared gel all over his head. First Nico gave him a Mohawk, later flattened out by my hands with the curly comb, then Nico resigns himself to just making two points on either side. We've tried out something like ten different coiffures by the time the end credits come on. Then my father thanks us, gets up, time for the afternoon snack.

On the table, the cake wrappers and jumbo-sized cereal boxes have labels, brightly colored circular stickers, yellow letters on red strips. I read the words on the packaging, knowing I've already read them in snack times gone by, but today something new has appeared amid the usual crispbreads and fruit tartlets. Who did mama buy this for, this box of thirty low-fat plum compotes + 30% free, family-size special offer?

Nico's mouth is full of cereal gone soggy from milk and salivation, he chews it and it becomes inedible. He looks at me with round eyes, no, he doesn't look at me, I serve as a visual support for his frantic mastication, like the TV. He swallows it all, represses a heave and plunges his spoon back into the bowl of milk to fish out the last yellow squares. I reach out and grab a pile of flyers that came in our mailbox. My father usually keeps the best ads for himself, the variety stores, and leaves us only the supermarkets, job lots, and dishware. This time I get the furniture stores, the high-end stuff.

I turn the pages, linger over the beds, the bookshelves, the armchairs. My father emptied his pockets on the table yesterday, small change, shopping cart tokens. A raclette maker is waiting for something to happen, stamped envelopes stand in as trivets and four telephones salvaged from the dump rub elbows with paracetamol tubes, a pair of tweezers, the remote, a measuring tape. I take care not to touch the edge of the table as I leaf through the flyer. When the sponge runs over the

43

Formica it sweeps crumbs down into the rim of the extension, it skips over the edges, I try not to think about it.

Nico gets up, dumps the milk into the sink, sets down his bowl. Wrapped in a comforter, his blankie, he walks out of the kitchen with Mickey Mouse. I'll soon be done with the furniture store, I've reached the multimedia section, and just then my father comes and sits down with fresh supplies from the kitchen. He takes advantage of my distraction to take away the furniture store, grabs the cereal box. I don't know what to eat. Some sort of cheese is waiting on a little plate. My father has almost finished the furniture and I know the home decor store will be next. I'm not going to let him triumph that easily. I put my hand on the flyer and slide it toward me, keeping my eyes on my father. He's talking to me, I'm not listening, he doesn't see a thing. My father is almost on the last page of the furniture, there's nothing more to read underneath, as he'll soon find out.

I see him lay a finger on some all-time low price, he looks up as if he wanted to tell me something but he doesn't say a word. He stares out the window, looks at the swaying branches of a distant poplar. His eyes dim as if someone had given them a poke, the blue's mixed with some other color, the hue that stays in the hairs of the paintbrush after it's been rinsed. Downstairs, the parrot starts whistling again.

Last chore of the afternoon. I close the trash-room door behind me so I can be alone with the garbage bags. They all smell the same here, I throw them wherever. My job is to put the main trashcan under the masher, press two buttons at the same time, and lower the handle. You have to be of age to mash the trash. I don't see the next ten minutes going by. Whenever I go into the trash room I'm struck by the silence. Out front, everything happens against a background of beeping fryers, online orders, the drinks machine asking for milk, for fruit. Everyone's constantly talking, the manas ask us about our doings past, present, and future. They assign missions, issue challenges, explain the best way to do this or that. We all tell each other what we're doing, what we have yet to do, we talk to the customers, here you are, go from table to table, how does our loyalty program work, it's very simple. In the trash room my ears ring, but it's a relief.

One day Chouchou asked a coworker if she wouldn't mind mashing the trash and the coworker answered no not at all, and she added, I like doing that. I glimpsed a flash of suspicion I'd never seen before in Chouchou's eyes. When the coworker went off to mash, Chouchou followed her to be sure she wasn't using her phone in the trash room.

—No, no, you don't have to be afraid, you just help yourself!

My father pulls a computer and a tablet from the dumpster. It's simple, you climb the gate at the dump and it's all yours. He adds, they only lock it for show, it's not to keep people from coming in, and anyway all this stuff has been tossed out, no one wants it anymore. We're inside the Berlingo and my father is filling the trunk. Who wants a tape player? Sylvie, come see the vacuum and the tablet, people will throw away anything, look Nico this is brand name, you can never have too many cables. A game with big buttons, he says people are crazy they're crazy. He gradually fills up the car and Nico chews at the nozzle of something or other while my father brings aboard a vacuum cleaner, a television. Someone's expecting us tonight and my father's swallowed up by the dumpster, all you can see is his legs sticking out. This is our lucky day, he says again and again, come see, but no one goes, everyone's waiting on the other side of the fence. One by one my father brings out the latest thing from years ago that he's going to fix up in our garage, the latest thing from years ago that he can boast about rescuing, and about how well it works, yes the PC's a little heavy but the screen lights up. At home we play on three different game consoles plugged into the batteries of the robots my father fixes at work.

Mama honks the horn. My father still doesn't come out, his body still immersed in the pile of junk he's tossing out far behind him. Another honk, finally he comes, a smile on his lips, his arms loaded with consoles and screens. The van starts off. Nico waves his hand and says bye-bye little dump, see you next week.

—You seem tired this afternoon.

I turn back toward Chouchou, blankly.

—What?

—I was saying you seem like you're miles away, what are you thinking about?

—You notice that water leak along the drive-thru hall? I was just wondering where it's coming from, you know?

Chouchou goes off for her break and it's time for me to clock out. In the changing-room bathroom I offer up a silent prayer to be spared the front room tomorrow, and then a second prayer, more realistic, to be spared noon to four thirty.

*   *   *   *

We're on our way to visit my grandparents and my aunt who can't eat by herself. I'm wearing the tunic top they gave me for my tenth birthday and all I can think about is afterwards, when we can go home. Nico mutters something and when I try to answer I realize that he's talking to the game console in his hands. In the car doors, tissues, a few CDs, and then the dog brush, the one that strokes the fur and never detangles it. The parents are talking. Mama combs her hair with her fingers, she's folded down the sun-visor mirror and she then turns around, look okay? I glance up and say yeah without seeing her, she asks Nico the same question and he doesn't look up, you're a dope Nico. I feel a little like throwing up, I'm thirsty but when I ask for water they hand me a bottle of warm Hépar. Mama's face disappears under a sweater and my father has turned down the radio. You can smell his cologne, his hair gel, the leather of his shoulder bag. He drives, Balavoine sings "Lady Marlène," the weekend gently goes by.

—Sorry, the drinks machine isn't working this evening. We can't serve you anything carbonated, all we can offer you is water, orange juice, and iced tea.

I repeat the same words to the customers sitting out front, the customers standing at the counter, the ones bent toward the drive-thru window even though that's not my station. I'm still out front. While Chouchou puts macaroons on plates I repeat that it's water, orange juice, iced tea, and then Chouchou comes over to tell me actually no, no iced tea either, we thought maybe but it comes out all strange. So I change my message to no, only water or orange juice, bottled sparkling water is fine, there we are, thank you thank you, bundle up tonight, my colleague will bring you your salad, no no that's not a piece of fingernail in your salad, it's the end of your wooden fork, you've broken it off, that's all, you can relax, you're welcome, you want extra sauce but you already have four packets of ketchup. Flat and sparkling water, I'm tired. It's eleven at night and I have to take a full tray of orange juice out to some girls sitting way in the back for a little privacy. They're the first to complain about the wait—so in that case sit close to the counter and yell instead of hiding away like you wanted to camp here, out of sight until we close. There you are, sorry sorry, please sorry.

A puddle of orange juice appears under my feet before I realize the tray's not in my hands anymore. Yellow sign caution slippery floor and I wring out a dishcloth, the customers around me wait for their mineral water while I try to steer the orange juice toward a floor drain, I fail. Chouchou says oh goodness and I want to rip out her blonde bun with my fingernails since she never tucks it away under a net, since it shamelessly flounces around in the face of our plastered-down hair in that mandatory prison. Chouchou asks if I want any help but she goes

47

away before I can answer, she shoulders her purse, she says see you girls, looking at an order kiosk. That's the trick, she never talks to anyone, she never looks at anyone. Chouchou is a sort of automaton that pops out every day for its routine.

The rooms in my grandparents' house disappeared as I grew. Things started to mount up, and then began climbing up the walls. The study disappeared, the bathroom too, the windows stopped opening. If you forget your scarf at my grandparents' you can't hope to find it again, not even the very next visit. I know my girlfriends are waiting for me to tell them my stories on Monday but all I can bring back from this place is the smile of a well-behaved, sad child. My father never fixes anything here, he knows it's all beyond repair, in the car he tells mama it's hereditary it's unbelievable and mama says shut up Jérôme, if you keep that up I'm going to open the door and jump out.

My grandmother asks what would you like to drink? and I answer water, just water, nothing in it. I don't want her to open the fridge, I'm sitting at the end of the table next to a six-foot stack of regional magazines, and I see the refrigerator door, a dirty gasket, the greasy smears, the old magnets. Water, that's fine. My grandmother smiles at me, her lips cling to her gums and she starts toward the refrigerator door, I say tap water. My grandmother doesn't hear very well, she softly walks over and pulls on the handle.

The drinks machine is still out. I'm like a little kid delighted by the breakdown, like when the electricity goes out and you have to light candles. A coworker has just come in and we don't have time to tell her it's not working. She pushes a button on the machine and suddenly everything goes berserk. A clear, vaguely tinted liquid explodes into the cups under the tap and the customers amassed at the counter all step back. The ones at the register wanting replacements for their ice-cold hamburgers duck behind the kiosks. Crew members throw themselves to the floor, hands over their heads to ward off shrapnel. Laura keeps saying calm down, it's no big deal, she limps to the machine and gives it a thump. No one dares complain anymore, everyone goes back to work and one crew member still crouched on the ground sets about cleaning a machine with a toothbrush. I've forgotten when I'm supposed to leave and the time clock isn't honking this evening, it's keeping quiet.

Only the raindrops hitting the car's roof enliven the trip home. We drive off from my grandparents' house and soon the shopping center comes into view. There's no connection between the things piled up at my grandparents' and the things in the supermarket aisles, all new, inoffensive. They don't smell like mildew, they don't smell like anything. My father sets the brake and mama slides open the back door. She says okay let's go, and then you sure you don't want to come? I shake my head. The mist mats her hair, she clasps the sides of her hood. My father's already far away, a coin in his hand to unlock a shopping cart. Nico makes up his mind to get out, the door slams shut and my mother walks off, holding my brother's hand. All the door locks click down.

I get a pen from the glove compartment and go on with the story I imagined at my grandmother's, which is mine alone. The heroine's name is Natacha, she lives in a cabin deep in the forest but comes home at night to sleep at her parents' house. Her mother is a psychologist, her father a writer or teacher. She has a pet, maybe a dog who knows her by heart, and also she wears red underwear, she doesn't have any friends because of that choice, and one day it's raining, she's out walking in an alley, and just when she's supposed to be hurrying some boys accost her, hey red, hey you red, she walks faster, her white T-shirt is see-through because of the rain and she finds herself on the ground, the boys are hitting her, they unhook her bra, I don't know if they end up running away, I'll have to decide, maybe her dog is a wolf dog, maybe her father comes to the rescue.

Later I transcribe the story onto the family computer prominently displayed in the middle of my parents' bedroom. The boys run away, Natacha is lying in the middle of the alley but her psychologist mother will understand her better than anyone, the wolf dog will show up, but the computer screen turns blue, I call for my father, I have to finish the story. Again and again he says I'll fix it, I picked it up at the dump, I know how to fix it, but the computer screen goes dark. My father puts in CDs, types in a few numbers and letters and I leave the room in dismay. A few hours later he knocks at my door and comes to me with a big smile, I reinitialized it, I have the whole thing saved on a disk. But when I go back to the computer the story I was writing is gone. I look in all the folders but only the photos escaped unharmed. My father keeps saying I fixed it I fixed it, my father keeps up his lie.

The door closes behind me, and the first thing I do in the locker room is take off my mask. I throw the hairnet into the big trash can and sit down, wiped out. I take a moment to pull off my shoe covers. A crew member is already getting into her clothes, she looks up, says hello. She gives me a glance, I know that look. I'm the crew member who never participates in anything, never joins anything, and never eats with anyone. The crew members know my oversized eyes above the mask but not my name, they wonder if I'm new here, or old, or a ghost. The girl changing clothes opens her mouth once, closes it, turns away, then declares, her eyes fixed on the pants she's putting on, a smile on her lips:

—This was my last day.

✳ ✳ ✳ ✳

One evening, as I'm trying to find the right junior internship, my father tells me there's one thing about work, you can't let it swallow you, you've got to stand up for yourself. He tells me

50

about his interview at the factory, the manager said shall we sign? and my father said I'll think it over, and he dares to ask is this a new position or a replacement? He's thinking about the mill, the constant turnover at Besnier-Charchigné. My father walks out of the factory with the roar of the presses ringing in his ears, tells himself I'll never come to work in this shithole.

I wrote up my CV and my cover letter with mama's help, my father read them over but didn't have any comments. He frowned and added watch out, there's more to life than work, you've got to have hobbies, passions, things you do on the weekend, and you can't let yourself get sucked in otherwise that's it. I don't understand what's it and my father says again watch out, watch out for work.

Great is my surprise when at noon I see my name written down for the restaurant's café. For several days I'd been complaining about the routine and Chouchou promised I'd have a better station but I was still waiting. Today I finally escape the front room and I'm determined to deserve it. I step behind the counter.

I knew that in this station you have to put macaroons on plates, make salads in bowls, do the washing-up, take the rolls out of the freezer and heat them. The café counter is colored chocolate and cream, to give it a homey feel. Your apron matches the drive-in's colors. To make coffee, you have to select it on a touchscreen and empty the grounds. Not long after I've started, Chouchou comes to join me, I know you were sick of the front so I fought to have you put here today, I used my influence, are you glad?

I soon realize that this station is Chouchou's hiding place and I'm a long way from salvation. The café space opens right onto the front room, there's no swing door between. A front-room crew member can easily handle the work in the café because there's nothing to do there, or almost. The counter I'm resting my elbows on is different from the one where the orders are assembled, further on. Here I'm not part of anything. I wait with a clean cloth over my arm, try to blend into the old-fashioned bar decor. The metal-rimmed coffee machine looks like a vintage jukebox. All the same, I'm reluctant to serve the ever-more-transparent liquid coming out of it. No, Chouchou says, it's okay like that. I get some macaroons and lay them out in the display case with a plastic glove while they thaw. I wait for the dishes and when Chouchou walks by I'm cleaning the cup drawers, there's nothing she can say to me.

The walls are thin in the apartment. I hear my father saying they have to see about other kinds of work, so they can get an idea, they have to meet different kinds of people, and the next day we go to the local library's first annual book fair.

We wait in the parking lot for the library to open. The car smells of the heater, the stray potato chips in the corners, the after-school *pain au chocolat* crumbs, it smells of the synthetic fabric of the headrests and the seat covers that have come off again, they always have to be put back in place. Nico is playing on his console and my father's listening to the radio a little too loud in the front seat, he's opened the window and his arm is hanging out the door. Mama's trying to talk to him. He keeps lowering the volume, repressing a sigh, then turns it back up when she stops talking, as if she weren't going to start in again. Mama's trying to finish a book she was supposed to turn back in days before. We're waiting for Charles, the librarian, his green Laguna always comes along from the same direction and always parks in the same spot.

Mama props her feet on the dashboard and my father takes out a four-year-old newspaper. Nico pushes his console buttons so hard that he has stamped the O key on his right thumb. Sound of a car, I turn my head, the Laguna's pulling into the lot. My father goes on reading his paper and mama gets out, posting herself at the library door before Charles comes along with his ring of keys. He takes his time, and when he reaches the door he announces that the writers aren't here yet, they're still at lunch.

Sitting in an armchair at the back of the library, books stacked on my knees, I picture them in a fancy restaurant, they must be hot in their suits, they share thoughts about their works, they discuss inspiration, they thank their parents and take another helping of fish. They wipe their mouths with very soft, very thick white napkins. Nico's reading a comic book, I don't know where the parents are. Whenever the front door bangs open I look up, but every time I see it's not the writers. Writers don't wear beach shorts and flip-flops, not to mention that writers don't have library cards, they write books, they don't borrow them. I find my father paging through *The Counts of the Pays d'Auge* and mama's trying to communicate with Nico. She whispers I want to have a talk with you about this morning, you were disagreeable, but I don't hear the rest. My father looks up, ah here they are.

A very diverse group of people is coming down the library hallway, laughing loudly, headed for the multipurpose room. Mama pulls Nico's arm, and my father follows. I ask him questions but he shrugs, they write books, that's all, what more do you need to know?

I enter the room where two rows of tables are facing each other. I don't know where to start, I put on a big smile and it stays on the whole time, I forget about my parents. I make for a table on the right. I don't ask questions, I don't say anything, I curiously look over the books they've laid out, with the distance I've learned so well, watch out they're going to try to sell you something. I'm almost on the defensive, because I'm not going to buy anything. Some of them talk to me but I don't understand much, I just smile, nod, and hand them the little notebook, hoping to collect their autographs. They laugh, they don't know what to write, and then they try to be witty and once the dedication is finished I read it over several times until I know it by heart, as if they'd let slip some sacred word,

53

something mysterious that would guide me in life: thanks for your interest in books, to the future great reader, to a charmer, from a volunteer fireman who gives you a big hug.

I don't really know why that fireman is there but he's there, he signs my book. I don't see that he's corrected the verb, that he wasn't sure just what form it should take. My parents are nowhere to be seen. I've stopped before a man who retraced his genealogy, someone who drew big piles of knots, now I'm standing in front of a calligrapher who's making me a bookmark for five euros, I'll ask mama for the money.

I'm a little warm. I clutch my autograph book to my chest and obstinately go on making my way around the table, I smile, I say hello, and then a writer refuses to sign, he stares into my eyes and says no. I turn around, Nico's far away, they've all gone off. The writer slowly pushes the notebook toward me, gives me a faint smile before getting hold of himself and putting on a serious air. He looks behind me, at someone, maybe another writer, and I'm no obstacle, he can see through me, I don't have a face. I turn around, Nico's far away and my parents are chatting with Charles, they didn't get anything signed. Without that last signature my notebook will be incomplete forever. I'll be missing a vital key. The writer quickly glances my way again, uneasy, he'll be glad to see me go on my way.

The table I've put my book down on isn't entirely clean, it's coated with a fine layer of grease since it was also used for bingo a few weeks ago, the baskets of fries grouped in the middle of the table so they wouldn't soil the cards. My father won the fanny pack and matching backpack last year. I didn't win anything, Mama bought me five cards and I put the red and green tokens on the wrong numbers, Nico was galloping around on all fours under the tables and then he smacked into the metal bar, the one the writer is resting his foot on today, his worn-down ankle joints in maroon socks, every day he must rest his foot on the same metal bar, from one book fair to the next. He pumps his foot on the bar. I know that in a few seconds he's going to pick up my autograph book between his fingers and hand it back to get me out of the way people who want to buy his book. He's going to hold it out to me but I don't feel like taking it, I want mama, Nico, and my father to come back, pay for the bookmark, and then we can all go away, I want the metal bar to snap under the writer's foot.

The oven door slowly opens and a nursery-school tune announces that the rolls can come out. Chouchou goes running. In the café space, I'm mired in the heart of pointlessness. I'm a living billboard for everything homemade, but all I do is push buttons. I take a pair of tongs and put a cookie in the customer's spoon to go with his coffee, Chouchou has taught me all there is to know, how to make frappés, heat the cinnamon rolls, and *pains au chocolat* in three minutes, but knowing a milkshake takes two shots of vanilla will never be of any use to me outside of here. I stick a straw into the whipped cream but don't take off the end of the paper wrapper so they'll know it hasn't been used, I'm conscientious. The rest of the time I swap commiserating glances with the crew member on multistation, another nonjob. She's behind the real counter but at the cash register, even though most of the customers pay at the kiosks. On multi, as in the café, daydreaming is as inevitable as it is forbidden, you always have to look busy.

I watch the multistation crew member disinfect her hands, blow up balloons, and restock the spoons in the drinks-and-desserts station in hopes of taking it over. She's waiting for the drinks crew member to run off for ice cubes, hoping to steal her station in her absence. More than once she gets a scolding from Chouchou, a customer has been waiting at the register for the past minute and where are you? dishing up ice cream? that's not your job. She'll try again later.

We avoid making eye contact with the other crew members breathlessly running around with trays in their hands, we'd like to help out but we're crew members in exile, kept away from the action and yet so close to the hustle and bustle of the counter. The rush never comes our way. I blow on the flies buzzing around the *pains au chocolat*.

Standing to one side, Jérôme watches Sylvie pay for our bookmarks. When the book fair is over, Jérôme offers to help fold the chairs, but when he realizes that the writers are clearing the tables and even washing the buffet dishes he flees, intimidated to get too close to them. He's checked out *The Counts of the Pays d'Auge*, and in the car he says can you imagine, those counts lived not too far from here, as if they were distant cousins and all he had to do was mention them to have a reunion.

Before dinner my father insists that we all go for a walk in the woods. Mama doesn't say much, picks up chestnuts and blackberries, she says it's cool out and then so did you like the fair? I nod, my mouth full of the blackberries they keep handing me. My father won't let it drop, you know one of those writers lives in La Ferté-Macé, I told him that's where you were born. And as we stroll down the muddy path, my father takes a pair of clippers from a pocket in his fleece vest and cuts off a bramble that's in the way. He prunes it as if he were out in his garden and came across a stray branch that was spoiling the effect.

I was helping out the crew member on drinks and was just about to take over her station so I could get out of the washing up when the Coke started spitting. Then the orange juice began yelling *refill refill* but nobody there spoke English, the manager said maybe it means, wait, I'll look it up, no I don't know. After the orange juice it was the iced tea and everyone was worried because the tea looked like the orange juice before it started yelling *refill refill*, the same look in the cup, and the Coke was still spitting away quietly. I take advantage of the chaos to take off my apron and make a milkshake like any other crew member with a job to do, but the machine won't let me.

—So you're at the ice cream machine, it's been beeping for a few minutes, and when you tried to make a shake scalding liquid splashed on your arms. Why do you suppose that happened?

—Because it's broken?

—Actually, no. When it beeps like that and you get the error message *shake fill*, that means it's out of milk, so you go to the posi to get some. You have to take care not to confuse the shake milk with the other milk but you'll see, it's a blue packet. While you're there you could even pick up a few pouches of chocolate and caramel because we're almost out, and then you get the little step stool, you open your shake milk with this, you put it over the cap and pry, then you pour the whole pouch into the compartment. Toss it into the garbage bag below and then push the button to tell the machine everything's set, but most of the time it stops as soon as you fill the milk, you got that?

—Which way's the posi?

＊＊＊＊

—You're Lebrac?

—I beg your pardon?

—Lebrac, in *La guerre des boutons*.

—Um, yes, what can I do for you?

—I'm a big fan, I saw that you live here and actually I live pretty close by, just a few miles away. I found your address on a site that talked about you, I mean I found it on the internet, but anyway, I really wanted to meet you.

—…

—So I brought my children, I'm always showing them *La guerre des boutons*, I hope I'm not being a pest. I brought some pictures for you to sign, they're stills from the film, I printed them out, you understand, so of course the color's not very good but, it's crazy how hard you are to recognize, when was that movie, sixty years ago? More?

57

—…

—We can always come back later, maybe this isn't a good time.

—No, no, come in, come in.

—Thanks! We don't get many movie stars around here.

—…

My father steps onto the doormat with a picture of a dog on it. The red bow on its head has gone pastel over the years. Lebrac has barely cracked open the door, just his head sticking out. My father pushes his way through, we go in, it's nicer in here than outside he says. A very surprised little woman comes in from the kitchen with a dishtowel in her hands. Lebrac mumbles something to her, goes and sits down on his couch but quickly gets up again, he seems to be lost in his own living room, not sure how to react. Nico merrily follows my father and I start down the red-tiled hallway timidly. My father talks and Lebrac takes the photos he's holding out, four pictures printed off the family computer. For the last one the ink was almost gone but it came out all the same. The pictures show a blond-headed kid glaring at the lens. In that scene he's defying another kid, whose buttons he's going to take. My father stands over Lebrac's shoulder as he signs the pictures. I meet Mme Lebrac's gaze, she asks if I'd like a snack cake and I hurry to decline, quietly, hoping she won't make the same offer to my father, who'd say yes to anything if it meant he could stay a little longer.

In the middle of the living room, a fireplace like at my grandparents', a sideboard, photos of grandchildren, postcards from the Île de Ré. His signatures completed, Lebrac holds out the pictures to my father, he says there you are. My father narrates his favorite scenes, when you say this, when you do that. Nico looks on, resting his elbows on something, he scratches his arm, yawns, Mme Lebrac offers him a cake too and he says no nicely, then, he almost forgot, quickly adds thanks. Lebrac says yes I was just a boy and my father gets down to business. He wants a photo with Lebrac.

Nico asks are we going home soon, but my father says this is our chance, he poses next to Lebrac, I'm behind the camera and I'm afraid he's going to put his hand on Lebrac's shoulder, I press the button seven times to be sure, flashbulb sound, I don't check that the pictures are good, okay let's go. Lebrac starts a sentence with well it was good of you to come but my father wants one more picture, maybe with the children. He puts his hand on Nico's shoulder, I keep my distance, and Mme Lebrac takes the camera, says if we ever have a chance to stop by again, and the door closes behind us. In the car, my father says nothing. When we get home he turns off the engine, he heaves a long sigh. Nico and I wait for him to say something and then he turns toward us, smiles: that was a good idea, going there.

—Explain this?

A manager reaches into a bag and takes out the meal a crew member has made for herself before going home. The mana stirs the ice cream with a wooden spoon, looks in the cup before banging it down on the counter and pointing her finger at the miscreant.

—Did you ask a manager if you could take this home?

She waits for an answer, I look on as I dry my washing-up with a paper towel. While I was gone fetching a caramel pouch the crew member on multi took over the dessert station. I've lost this round of musical chairs, I go back to the macaroons in the café space. I hear the crew member stammering I don't know but the manager says of course you know, everyone knows that, everyone but you for some reason, and this isn't the first time. I cut myself cleaning the mixer but I can't put my finger in my mouth, I think she's going to get off, put her meal on a tray and be done with it, but the manager hasn't finished yet. All around, the customers are waiting for their orders, the crew members are still running around except a few who've stopped to watch the scene so they can tell the people who weren't here about it later. The manager starts in again.

—Did you ask someone if you could have two flavors and put an extra cookie in your ice cream?

I turn around again. The manager's name is Caro. She has a splint on her wrist, rectangular glasses, purple hair. Her face is wide, she wears a lot of eye makeup, and you always know it's her even if you don't see her: she's the only one who yells, the only one who can't tolerate chatting crew members. Caro's pointing at the melting ice cream. She's terrifying because she's unpredictable, she can stand there like that forever. She snatches the bag and shakes it in the crew member's face and says so, so so so, and then she hands down the sentence.

—You're going to redo your ice cream and you're going to eat it here, that's what you're going to do.

Caro throws the cup of two-tone ice cream into a counter trash can. The whole room breathes a sigh of relief.

My father tacked up the pictures Lebrac signed in our apartment along with the ones we took at his house. He set aside the photos where someone blinked or moved unexpectedly. Except one, where, next to my father who's holding Nico's shoulder, Lebrac's mouth is open. His mouth makes a perfect o, as if in silent protest. My father put that one up in the middle of his exhibition. Lebrac isn't smiling in any of the ten photos.

I finished a salad in 160 seconds. The screen that tells me what to make next shows the seconds in red, starting at 199 and counting until I touch the screen displaying the order, we call that bumping. The countdown stops after 999 seconds, and the box stays red, you can't make a customer wait longer than fifteen minutes. A crew member comes to pick up my salads as soon as they're ready.

I decided to drink all the smoothie dregs and for the past few hours I've poured what's left in each mixer into a cup, and

I vanish into the drive-thru hall. Crew members run across it now and then, bringing an order. I keep going, and behind the cardboard boxes I find the leak again, my feet in the water, I'm back where I left off. Here and there the flood swells, like it was caught in a trap, and going on I reach the drive-thru prep area, where the orders are assembled after they've been relayed on the headset. The leak is coming from the drinks machine at this station, the one the crew members revert to when the other one breaks down. The machine is buzzing softly, like a giant insect. I abandon my investigations, I wade back toward my station.

Out front, the guilty crew member is eating her ice cream, the regulation mix this time, she's on her phone, smiling, nothing happened. Caro is chatting with Laura, their elbows on the order assembly table, a sort of nook where the burgers come out on a conveyor belt from the kitchen. The table is heated by big lamps, the crew members take what they need from it to fill out their orders. My colleague on multistation doesn't look at me anymore, doesn't smile with her eyes anymore.

I dream that someone is whispering in my ear, it's time you can go now. I dream of whispered words but everyone's talking loudly. The orders slow down, the boss puts his jacket on because he's about to leave, the managers turn on the terrace lights, the crew members ready themselves for the assault of the night.

DEEP FAT

Change of stations at lunch today, I'm on fries. The others wish me courage and the trainer reappears, here we go again. Four and a half hours ahead of me, I put on the plastic apron, I'm all set.

They give me the instructions: when the beeps are slow and strident that means shake the baskets, short and urgent means take the fries out of the oil. Other buzzers go off, but they say those aren't a big deal, just push this button. I glance at the order screen just above my head, I don't read it, I can see there are too many orders, I push the button. Frozen rectangles fall into the basket. I pick it up, my wrist twists, I lower the fries into the oil and the countdown begins. The crew members behind me say faster now, pick up your output, come on, speed it up.

Fry scoop in hand, I fill the cartons, dredge the trays, but the alarms stop me, I drop everything, answer the call. I push the button, the buzzer stops, I shake the basket, I put in a new one and I'm at peace for four seconds, now validate, twenty seconds, now shake, three minutes, now take out the fries. A crew member chides me why are you putting down the scoop, I want to see it in your hand till you've filled all your orders. I'm not alone with my fries anymore, they're watching over my work, from the way I hold the scoop to the movements of the baskets, I have to keep it moving. Pick up the tool, fill, the cartons go off as soon as they're ready, I tamp fries into

63

bags, into cartons, I'm losing ground, the orders are piling up. Someone tells me the thing is you have to put in the next one as soon as you take out a basket, you see? Snap, snap, you get that? So why aren't you doing it?

Buzzers, slow, two together, fast, at first I'm not sure, are those the fryers buzzing or the fish fillets further down the kitchen? After a while I figure it out, the noise comes from my chest like when the bass makes it vibrate, like when I used to put my little-girl hand to my heart thinking it was going to explode to the sound of "Les démons de minuit." More alarms, online orders flash on the dashboard behind me, my hands are too greasy, the noise is wearing me down, I shake the basket, let it go, pick it up again, buzzer, whirl around, the scoop with the bag at its end, the basket hung up over the vats, drain, shake gently, the oil spatters and pinches my forearms, all right, that will do, you're not supposed to spend hours on it, I empty it, toss it away with the others. The customers who send back their fries because they're not hot enough, I long to plunge their hands into the boiling oil, my own are red, the salt scratches.

A crew member needs a medium fry quick and I make it. Thanks medium fry! They still don't know my name. I tamp, I shake, finally I let go. Alarm, that means shake shake shake but no time. Someone pushes the button for me, violently shakes the basket to rebuke me for not doing it, and the others come back. They say the thing is you have to, but I'm not listening, yet another lesson's coming and I don't have time. Behind my back the boss is singing *on ira tous au paradis, on ira*.

Home after a night shift, Jérôme finds an official letter from the factory in the mailbox: he's going to get the *médaille du travail*. He wonders why nobody told him, sometime in the past few hours, why they didn't give him the letter in person. The envelope ripped open, the letter read, Jérôme puts it on the stack of flyers. He sits down at his bowl of cereal and waits for the house to wake up, pondering the best way to announce the news. Sunbeams filter through the curtains, lighting up the crumbs on the salmon-colored tablecloth. Jérôme hears the pipes vibrating from the neighbors' flushing toilet, hears the parrot wake up, hears their doors opening and closing toward eight in the morning. I join him in the living room, I don't know how long he's been waiting.

He tells me what's in the letter before I even have it in my hand. The ceremony will be a few weeks from now, but they won't cast the medal until later, that's only normal, making it takes time. They've already booked the restaurant, at the château, you know, we drive by it all the time, they run a hotel there too. We'll be on the ground floor, it ought to be good, anyway it's expensive. My father talks with his downturned smile, uncomfortable. He's trying to fend off an intrusive pride and go back to his usual serious self, but he can't fight it. I know that smile. He had the same smile the day we were in the car on vacation and he said you know I was a stillborn, the umbilical cord was wrapped around my neck and I wasn't breathing.

Nico answered that's impossible, that doesn't happen. My father insisted, oh yes, I was dead and they brought me back. One jolt of electricity got me going again. Nico put the console down on his lap, a little annoyed. Talking to my father's eyes in the rearview mirror, he said no, that's a lot of crap. The van stopped at the corner and my father raised his voice to put an end to the conversation, to silence all doubts. You don't need much to be reborn when you're a baby, that's all. And as we moved on to another subject he murmured, I think I could have died, yes. That's when that smile appeared.

I don't know if I'm supposed to congratulate him. My father wants an opinion, pretty good, don't you think? Of course, it's the least they can do, a little gratitude after twenty years with the same outfit. He puts a spoonful of cereal in his mouth, turns up the radio. I want to ask a question but he keeps me from it, slurping the milk from his spoon, he adds you know one day they offered me a promotion, an office job. I look at his dirty hands, I'm losing patience, so what happened? Nope, he says, not interested, I know guys who changed jobs, turned into suits overnight, you see them in the hallways. My father breaks off, raises his head, narrows his eyes, glances downward. He pretends to button a suit jacket, stands up, mimes a silent walk, looks me up and down, then goes back to his normal face, I swear that's just how they are.

A cloud of oily steam envelops me with every basket I put in. The customers can watch the whole process from their tables: this is the only kitchen station you can see from the front. I sort the bags by size, small, medium, large, while next to me crew members armed with sauce pistols flip burgers, wrap them, slide them toward the central conveyor belt. A manager shouts low on wrappers and a supply person answers, thanks wrappers. No one cooks here, what we do is guarantee a high temperature, a suitable appearance, conforming to what the customer already knows or might have tasted in another outlet of the chain. We operate food-production equipment, and our moves are the same moves crew members made twenty years ago.

After two hours on fries I know to dodge the crew members behind me picking up the bags. I anticipate their movements and their needs. Some of them talk looking straight at me to get their five large fries. Others don't say a word to me the whole shift. I don't know which I prefer. When I empty a basket into one of the three trays I say hot fries and all the crew members stand back. I've come to anticipate the buzzers. A crew member asks how long before the next fries and I say two and a half minutes without even looking at the timer. Another refills my fridge so I'll never run short. I settle into a frantic rhythm: take the basket out, put the basket in. I always press on the alarms with my middle finger. My hands are used to the temperature. I hold out the cartons and the crew members say fuck that's hot!

I don't know what I look like. My forehead is the only part

of my face they can see, they gauge my state by that patch of skin, its creases and furrows, the knitting of the brow just below, but they don't see my eyes. My eyes are glued to the fryer, and the heat lamps make two suns inside them. My mouth is open under the mask, it never closes. Concealed by the cloth, it grants itself that liberty.

The crew member on drive-thru makes me a drink, she says I'll just leave this right here. The orders slow down, I take the cup and walk away a few steps to drink while a colleague restocks my bags. The crew members always gather around the fryers, they strive to fulfill the desires and needs of the person working the oil, as if to make amends a little. Some wish me courage, they know my hands are scoured by the salt and I haven't had a thought for hours but all I want is to stay where I am. I'm not hoping for the drive-thru anymore, that's been taken over by the veterans and overtime takers, and all I'm afraid of is the front room and the emptiness it creates inside me. On fries everything's robotic, it stops me from thinking.

We don't know if we're early, if we're late. The door to the van slides open and the cold pours into the back. Have a nice trip? No trouble finding the place? Nico puts on his down coat, zips it up and climbs over me to get out, as if an important mission lay ahead. He pays me no mind and his tennis shoes leave dirty streaks on my pantyhose. I'm always the last one out. We wordlessly crunch over the gravel up to the half-inflated balloons taped to the community center door. In the entryway, a rack is sagging under the coats. No Smoking on the walls. White tile and a square of parquet in the middle for dancing, that's it.

The organizer is standing on a chair, tacking a few more balloons to the ceiling under the guidance of other guests. The tables form a U, and when I walk around it I discover my name on a business card in Vivaldi font pinned to a plastic cup. A few letters are missing on the happy birthday banner. I look for a place to hang out.

Nico and I tour the room, checking the storage areas off to the side until we find what we're looking for, the extra tables and chairs stacked up in a precarious sculpture. From our post we can see the room and the little stage where the DJ is plugging in cords and adjusting the lights.

The dishes are served, the parents talk, the kids run around the tables under the blinding lights. They say tag you're it, grab each other, and my father says there'll be tears in two minutes. We hear a bang and a parent leaps up. At dessert time the guests queue for their piece of cake on a paper plate. On the buffet there are a few dishes left on the buffet, a three-quarters-eaten Piedmontese salad, a few cornichons from what was once a charcuterie platter, a chicken carcass in a greasy puddle.

Someone's knocked over a glass of water, the paper tablecloth is torn here and there. The table runner is a mess. The gaily colored napkins are crumpled beside half-eaten pieces of bread and toothpicks from the appetizers. At the far end of the U, I see my father pointing at his chest, one finger on the upper right of his sweater, making a circle, the medal, that's all he's been talking about for days, the *médaille du travail*. I can't hear him but I know what he's saying, twenty years on the job that's something to celebrate, no seriously things are good, I'm not complaining, it was worse back at Besnier. Mama looks at the lights playing over the wood floor, the DJ uses his microphone to congratulate, invite, remind. My father drones on, the ceremony's in a week, we'll be eating in a château, the one you see when you're coming to our place, just across from the police station, you know the one, right? Which way do you come? Mama would like to dance, she's got her chair turned toward the dance floor but she doesn't get up. The DJ repeats don't be shy, don't be shy, and my father has to raise his voice. He gesticulates with his hands, in any case what really matters is. I can't make out the rest. His audience nods, they heard. My father is smiling his clenched smile of happiness. He bends down to pick something up and disappears. Mama still wants to dance but can't find the moment, the DJ says last song and she stands up but no, it's a slow dance. Couples open their arms.

Mama gets up, heads toward our paper-wrapped tower. We've been found out, Nico's getting ready to run but I stay where I am. My father is still bent over and I don't know what it is that really matters, I didn't catch the end of his sentence. Mama reaches me, maybe it won't be much longer, she's holding her coat, she never danced. Back at the tables, my father straightens up, his bag strapped on tight.

It's been a few minutes since somebody wanted fries. The last ones I took out, in anticipation of a rush without end, are waiting patiently in the trays. A kitchen crew member comes over and opens a burger box, a withered garnish is quivering inside. Look, here's something you'll never see again. He explains that every day someone orders a burger no bread and toy single. The words come out of his mouth in the machine's order.

I'm about to wash my fry scoops when Chouchou comes to see me. For a few days she's been lurking behind the counter, telling everyone there aren't enough people out front, the situation's complicated. She recounts the latest incident with the Romas from across the way. The guy threw that little girl against the order kiosk, can you imagine, I can't deal with it anymore, I need reinforcements, it's impossible. I generally avoid making eye contact, it's not hard, I have work to do or I find some. But today my fridges are full, my baskets are sitting in their places, the fryers have all been drained and I've taken care to wipe down the rims and scrub the stainless. I can't absorb myself in washing the scoops, she blocks my way before I've even reached the sink.

She says it's been a long time since we had a talk, asks a few questions then picks up a fry from one of the three trays. I'm expecting her to lower her mask and eat it, I've seen coworkers foraging after a rush, eating extra burgers in the drive-thru hallway, hunched over boxes, ready to hide the food if a mana appears. Chouchou turns the fry between her fingers but cuts it in two, looks at it crushed between her thumb and index finger.

—See honey, your fries are no good. They're too old, you're going to have to throw them all out.

The ceremony's tomorrow, and Jérôme has already picked out the shirt he'll be wearing. It's waiting on a hanger along with his suit pants. Today he's on afternoon, so he's slept in. He had lunch with us, played the recorder with his nose and started in on a harmonica song. Nico gets out the combs but dad says I have to go in an hour, I need to hurry. At the factory, he has to change his clothes again in the locker room, scan his badge, go up fifty feet in a cherry picker, come down again, walk, walk, wait for a call.

He has a little time to lark about with his coworkers and then the call comes, service request at the other end of the factory, on a safety catch he's forever having to repair. He puts on a helmet and adjusts his ear guards. The noise from the presses makes his head spin. The regular rhythm of the machines seems to keep time with his footfalls. He puts one steel-toed safety shoe in front of the other, they weigh tons. Some of the guys say hello to him on the way past if they have time. Sometimes they want to talk, but Jérôme keeps on walking. The sooner he gets there, the sooner he can go back to the office, take a break. Finally he reaches the robot, examines it, checks the safety catch several times. He doesn't understand.

—There's nothing wrong with your safety.

—Yeah, yeah, it works, but there's a screw missing.

—Are you kidding me?

—What do you mean?

—You're calling me about a missing screw? Electricity's got nothing to do with that, and you've got the supply people thirty feet away!

—Don't ask me, they told me to call maintenance!

70

—Look, you know my name perfectly well, I've been working here for three months, and I'm not going to throw these fries away. They came out ten minutes ago, throw them away if you like, but I'm not going to do it.

Chouchou doesn't answer. She looks away, as if this exchange never happened, as if her order had become moot. She leaves me with my bad fries and heads back out front, berating a crew member along the way. Taking out trays has priority! Everyone knows they have to do that, so how come you can never remember? Chouchou's found another target.

I push on a timer. The drive-thru crew member gives me a smile me because she's waiting for the fries to finish her order. I know I'll be at this same station tomorrow and I pray that the day after finds me here again and keeps me away from the front room forever. As long as the other crew members see me on fries, it'll become me, that'll be my place.

Through the wall I can hear my father raise his voice. It's incredible, they treat my crew like we're nothing at all. My face is turned toward the phosphorescent stars. Mama goes shh, my father starts up again. That guy had no idea, he said next time I just won't call. I was this close to blowing my top.

I have school tomorrow, I should have been asleep two hours ago. I don't really understand why, but I'm always waiting for my father to come home from work, I don't do it on purpose. I try going to bed earlier, I try to convince myself he probably won't be home until morning, but I can never drift off until I hear the door click, the keys jingle. I hear mama getting up, going to my father as he takes off his shoes in the entryway, no no don't touch me, don't touch me, I'm filthy. Then the answer, I can kiss you at least can't I Jérôme, and the rest is drowned out by the sound of the faucet, my father washing his hands.

In my bed, I relax my arms, my legs, I imagine I'm lying in the middle of an armored tank, out of reach.

—What about the cherry picker?

Mama's words come through, and my father heaves a sigh. My bedroom wall doesn't exist anymore.

—I don't give a damn about the cherry picker, I tell you that's the least of my troubles. I can put up with a lot, but all this back and forth, you can't imagine. They push you right to the edge, physically. But all the same I'm never mean, you really have to push me to make me turn mean.

Forehead against steel, I repeat the same moves over and over. Behind my back, everyone's on edge this lunch shift, we're expecting a crowd. My hands touch down in the usual places, start their itinerary over again, nothing ever happens. The fingers grip the baskets' plastic handles. The wrists bend at the usual angle to dump the fries into the trays. I salt, mix, open the carton by putting my thumb underneath and widening the gap with my index and middle fingers. They tell me that's not the best technique, they tell me you're filling them too full, don't put in so many. Slightly bent forward, back hunched, forehead against steel, I repeat.

A mana comes and stands next to me and doesn't pick up any fry cartons, says good job at lunch today and I answer a minute and a half more. Another minute and a half and no sign of activity on the screen. Out front, the crew members are vying to take out the last trays before the nothingness begins. Relief in the kitchen, and out front the hard part's just starting. Soon I'll press on the timer, pour out the last basket, clean my fingerprints off the fry scoops and my forehead-print off the steel. I'd like to undo the straps knotted earlier on my plastic apron, but after five hours I can't untie anything. I wait for someone to say okay that's enough you can go home now and already the flashbulb sounds come from the time clock, crew members punching out. Further on, I see Chouchou sitting down the way you can out front: cleaning a table, she pretends there's a hard-to-reach spot and takes a seat on the banquette so she can scrub more effectively. Microphone around his neck, the crew member on headset comes prowling about my frozen fries and the boss goes back to his office to count up the take.

The last fries go off, I grab and lift. My arm stretches out, my wrist locks to hold it high and straight and out front the customer watches me walking toward his table, his mouth watering, his hands glued to the banquette. I slowly lower the tray, hoping my wrist will hold up. Victory, I give a little smile invisible to the naked eye. I end up lecturing him to avenge myself for my trouble, please leave your tray on the table once you're done, it's easier for us, we have to know which tables are contaminated. The second tray on my other wrist is getting heavy and I leave the customer there, I've got to go do the same thing again further on.

At the fries station I tilt the basket so the oil will dribble back into the vat, and the boss inside my head is warning me, oil is the most precious thing we have here, we get all we can out of it and we don't waste a bit. The boss is training me to fill vats and for a moment he becomes the crew member he was way back when. He takes out the oil jug, balances it on a basket, there you see, you have to wait till there's not a single drop left, then you put it in the boiler room with the trash cans. He's fond of telling me he started at the very bottom. And I wonder, do the managers ever think about that? Is that what Chouchou thinks about when she takes the buns out of the oven, that she might go from manager to boss and how? Once the oil's drained out, I try to leave the basket resting on its hook, but I miss. It slips and I see the accident before it happens, it falls into the oil and it's back to the front room with me. No, I don't see anything, the screens have put my

73

brain to sleep. My arm reaches out over the vat, I block the fall, the sizzling hot basket lands on my hand.

An hour before he sets off for the ceremony, Jérôme wants to wash his hands. He asks Sylvie where the nail brush is and goes at it. The stiff bristles scour his fingertips, where black arcs have formed. My father scrubs, but the stains are permanently imprinted. He scrubs harder but only the dead skin comes away, the black stays behind and Jérôme says again and again it can't be it can't be. He loses patience, he's got to be going. He turns the tap on too hard to rinse the brush and sprays his violet shirt, he dries himself with a bathrobe. He still has to polish his shoes and the stains won't come out. Jérôme's losing heart, all the things he unscrewed and greased, all the things he repaired the day before, and now the stigmata, impossible to wash away. He comes out of the bathroom to find Sylvie and says I can't go like this. Hunched over the sink, Sylvie rubs Jérôme's hands like a stained garment. Jérôme keeps saying I'll never have time to polish my shoes and I'm going to get dirty, I'm disgusting, I can't go, I have to change shirts, no I can't go like this, it's all ruined, it's ruined. Sylvie doubles down on his hands but Jérôme is already looking away, abandoning himself there in the bottom of the sink.

In the managers' office they say did you rinse? At first I think they're talking about cleaning a station, doing the washing up, then I realize they're pointing at my hand. They add we can't give you cream, it's not allowed, but go to the tap and we'll get you a pair of gloves.

My hands under the water, I replay the scene in my head, my hand under the basket, where it wasn't supposed to be. For a moment I'd forgotten what the drive-in has taught me: anything that falls stays on the floor, anything that falls is already forgotten, it doesn't exist, it's useless. I moved before

I could think, I tried to stop a slippage and a disappearance. The tool hand resisted.

Jérôme walks into the restaurant to find the bosses already gathered at one end of the table, hands on the awardees' files. At the other end, his coworkers are chatting about the upcoming local fishing tournament, how much it costs for a spot, got to get there earlier this time. The talk turns to union-sponsored holidays, I managed to get Senegal this year, well, not me, it's the same every time. Jérôme lays his jacket over his chair back, takes the last petit four and a boss raises his glass. After the applause, the dinner comes out.

Jérôme thinks about the story he'll tell when he gets home. First he'll describe the heavy curtains, the old parquet floor, the thick napkins. He'll use an adjective, sweet, they didn't hold back, that's for sure, it was sweet. Then he'll answer our questions before we can ask: I had the fish. A great big fish, he'll specify, with swirls of sauce on the platter, round eye, gold scales, the bones plain to see, I didn't fork up a single one, it was so perfectly done. As for the rest he won't recall, he'll say I'm not quite sure anymore, maybe red mullet, in any case it was huge.

When the meal nears its end and the bosses shake the employees' clammy hands, Jérôme has stopped dreading going home empty-handed, without even a medal case to show off. It comforts him to know what he's going to say.

DRIVE-THRU

—You sure there's nobody home? I don't want to intrude.

   —No, there's nobody there, they're at work.

   —Both of them?

   —My mother's at her school, my father's at his office. When we get there I'll look and see if there's a car in front and then we'll know.

   —And if there is we'll go away?

   —Not necessarily. I'll ask if you can come in.

   —I don't want to intrude.

I walk down the sidewalk, and when we get to a gray gate Paul holds me back with one hand. This is it. For a moment I'd forgotten why we were walking there. A mailbox is attached to the gate, his last name above it. The letters are printed in a special font, not scrawled on a scrap of paper. Paul twists around to look through the horizontal gap in the privacy panel. You see, there's nobody here. I can't see anything, just barely a red-tiled rooftop, like in the south, when I look up.

—Where are you for lunch?

My smile answers for me. A glove on my hand, I make my way toward the reward, the vindication: drive-thru duty. The boss claps me on the shoulder, I'm his protégée, his warrior. Careful, he says again, let's not forget anything, and I nod. My station for weeks to come is riding on this lunch shift. While another crew member takes orders on headset, the one

77

on drive-thru duty organizes every step as an order's made up, drinks, desserts, fries, packing the bag. Contact with customers is limited. All you have to do is open the window, hold out the order, just long enough to be polite and be thanked by the customer, then close it again. Veterans and overtime workers earn the right to stay there. Everyone else has to fight for it, or to be hurt badly enough to be thought incapable of anything else. No harm comes to your hands when you're on drive-thru duty.

The drinks machine fills the first cups, I pick up a bag and with a brisk snap make it three-dimensional. I delight in the violence of that move, it's a release. I do the ice cream, the drinks fill, I add napkins, sauces. The hot stuff isn't there yet, a crew member puts it on my table, he says number one! and off it goes. Another order piles on, no time. I check the hot food, the sauces, add more, and open the window.

A cool breeze rushes in and ruffles my stack of napkins. Hello, here you are. I'm always afraid the customer will miss the bag and it will crash down outside the car, I don't let go until they close their fingers. Thank you, have a good day, goodbye, stay safe. I'm happy for four seconds, then another bag, napkins, sauces. A few crew members try to muscle in, hoping to take over the station, to score points. They say got your ice cream? can I do your ice cream? No, I answer, no I've got it. The crew member has already run off toward the machine. On the next order I start with the ice cream. Got your ice creams? Yes. All of them? The next five orders' ice creams are all done, they're going to melt, too bad. I want to win this game on my own. My opponent's not giving up, she asks if I have the donut for the fourth order and I hurry to fetch it, I get the espressos poured before they've even been paid for, over on headset. No sooner has the customer spoken the words large black in my coworker's earpiece than it's half full already. The five bags are there in front of me, ready for the hot stuff to go in, no one can stop me.

The boss asks me how I'm doing, I'm triumphant. I fend off

all the others, a crew member starts to unfold a bag for an order and I rip it from her hands, I snap excuse me the way you'd bark fuck off. While I'm getting my bag back, some other cow puts the lids on my drinks, I want to shove her into the sauce boxes, I tell her I can handle this you know. I go so far as to fetch the burgers from the assembly table before they can bring them to me, all the while making sure nobody takes the opportunity to wipe down my station with a counter cloth.

Chouchou is lurking, she starts to say you know I pulled strings to get you this spot. I don't look at her, we're not of the same world anymore, I've taken a step up. I pull the lever on the ice cream machine, it shakes, it might explode at any moment, it cuts off her words. Then I open the window, hold out the order, but when I turn around again the boss is looking at me with a raised eyebrow, a bag of hot stuff in his hand

—Forgot the four fries with your order, didn't you?

Paul enters a code with his right hand to open the gate, hiding the numbers with his left, out of habit he tells me, it's just a habit. He pushes the gate and my feet start down a paving-stone path. A little decorative garden has the right to grow around it. People were paid to put a fountain in here, an arch and climbing plants there, and little spotlights that turn on when it gets dark. But I only have eyes for the house that sits in the middle, the wide windows, the white linen curtains. They're linen, no doubt about it. The steps, what are the steps made of, marble or tile, sophisticated tile, salmon-colored tile, a little slippery. There's a banister, they foresaw that it would be slippery, they said when it rains it'll get slippery and they had a solution and they had the means. The curtains upstairs are translucent but they hide the inside. The walls are immaculate, a lantern hanging from a hook beside the front door, purely ornamental, no bulb inside.

At the front door, five steps above the ground, I turn around. To my right, the driveway, white pebbles, not dirty gravel. The pebbles are clean, some slightly tinted, hints of pink. The pebbles won't make furrows when the cars drive over them. They'll make way of their own accord, with none of that horrible crunching-gravel sound. The gate is surrounded by sensors, red diodes that never go out. You coming? Affixed to the royal blue door, a gilded knocker makes its presence felt. It's even with my nose, in the middle of my face. Paul takes out his key after patting his back jeans pocket, he turns it twice in the lock and shoves the door open with his shoulder, a sharp clack, forced entry. For a moment my hand lingers on the banister, you coming? I find the courage to put my feet on the broad doormat. He closes the door behind me.

And then, suddenly, framed family beach photos, a wall-mounted varnished key rack, he hangs his up on it, a built-in cabinet, two doors, the first one half open and inside white cloth storage bins, labels in metal rectangles, paracetamol, homeopathy. You can take off your shoes if you like. A metal stool at the foot of a cabinet, pegs and hooks to hang coats on, little wooden table, a mirror with transparent edges, a trinket tray, a few hair bands. I tug at the fat knot on my shoe, you thirsty? Loyalty cards from stores I've never heard of, a prescription. I have a quick look at it, what problems could they possibly have? I don't know what's in the fridge but we'll see. I look up. I was saying, you thirsty? It's ten, we've got to hurry. A quick glass of water, then.

The boss bends toward a crew member, whispers go help out at drive-thru duty, going to need a hand there. She comes and readies my fries, puts spoons in my ice creams, unfolds my bags, you remember the napkins? and I don't have the strength to refuse. I apologize to the boss, sorry, sorry Antoine. It's all over, I'm nobody's protégée now. Chouchou walks by with her bun and I know that tomorrow she'll pull strings to have me put back out front.

Left-hand room, windows on every wall. A big wooden table in the middle, fully fitted kitchen, trash can that opens when you walk past. We've got guava juice if you like. Windowed door to a veranda, stairs down to the yard, Australian shepherd. Unless you'd rather just have water. Huge china cabinet, a sort of dressing table, I don't have the words. Big mirror, photos stuck into the frame, papers in neat stacks. We have guava juice if you like. Why not. How do they keep their white floor tiles clean? We've got to hurry. They must have a good vacuum cleaner. I love you you know. He puts a glass down in front of me. Saffron tablecloth with geometric designs, I love you too. Sober vase, a few flowers inside, still fresh, chest of drawers behind the door, what on earth do they put in there, more papers, labels, I can't make out what they say. What do you think? Beautiful. No, I mean the guava juice. I think it tastes like dirt.

A door slams, I jump. He says it's just a draft and I put the glass in the sink. On the refrigerator door, more prescriptions held up by magnets, loads of business cards. You can put your glass in the dishwasher. The dog barks and when I stop at the French door to join him I see another house in the garden, another house behind the house, so two houses, one in front, one in back. Big French doors in the front of the second house, unless it's just an extension of the first house and not a separate house of its own? Or a storehouse, an annex under construction? Through the door I see an exercise bike, it really is a house, a house in the yard, not a shed.

—That's for guests.

—You don't have a foldout couch?

Another slamming door. We can't take long, it's a fifteen-minute walk to the lycée. I glance at the clock, half past, come on. I end up in a living room and he says this is the living room. On the left a white staircase going up and beside it three doors, another little table that serves no purpose, a gilt-edged mirror above it, fake clutter, a fibbing clutter, real clutter is coated with dust and bits of fluff. They don't know the first thing about clutter. A few magazines, a desk, imposing furniture, an interesting lamp with a bunch of white leaves clustered around the bulb, okay okay nobody's going to see your bulb. Plush carpet, armchairs, leather couch, collection of remotes on the oak coffee table, one for the TV, four for the players. I'm sure they all have their batteries. Flat screen, home theater, he says. It's thirty-five past and he says this is my father's home theater. I look at him, befuddled.

—I beg your pardon?

—DVD cabinet's over there, and this is my father's home theater.

—Why are you telling me this?

—I don't know, I thought it would interest you.

—Why would I be interested in your father's home theater? I don't even know what that is.

—Well, I'm showing you around, that's what you're supposed to do with visitors.

—What, you think I'm going to buy it?

—No, I don't know, I just wanted to show you where I live, I didn't think it was going to be some big deal.

—What is your problem?

Paul stammers, he pulls on a little flap of skin where his palm is scraped and puts his other hand on the couch. The leather is crumbling, white synthetic particles drift down onto the rug. Outside a car honks. The curtains aren't linen.

For the third time a door shuts and I hear footsteps, someone's on the stairs. Come on, he takes my hand, it nestles into his scraped palm. Time to get going. We head into the foyer, beach photos, hairs coiled around elastic bands, reminder, appointment at the hospital. I pick up my shoes by the laces, I clench my fist. In the kitchen, a fly buzzes against a window, the fridge is too loud, how did that fly get in here? Around me, the house seems to shrivel up like a wild gourd in the spring and a voice resounds from the stairway, someone says is that you? He opens the door to the veranda, he says we'll come back later. The Australian shepherd wags its tail and it smells good on the veranda, it doesn't smell like cellar or dog, it smells like something synthetic, vanilla, soap, and I hate them. He slams the door behind me and I run over the white pebbles, which turn dirty from my shoes.

✳ ✳ ✳ ✳

When the Italian car horn sounds I decide to go home. The time clock tells me it's late. In the locker room I sit down, my feet in the puddled water. A telephone rings in the locker room but there's no one to answer, it's a hopeless appeal. I take off my uniform and the last few hours at the drive-thru play in my head. The pace has picked up, the crew members have deserted their stations, and everything slips from my hands but I can't catch anything. Just when I knocked over a pile of paper napkins, Laura showed up.

—You're hopeless, your hot bags aren't closed right and you're too slow with the customers, it's ridiculous. Watch me.

Laura opens the window with a bag in her hand.

—Hello, here you are, goodbye. See? Nothing more. I'll put your bags together, all you have to do is pass them, you're way behind.

—Thanks.

On the fries screen, *27 more pending* announces a rush that will never end. Quitting time has come for me but everyone looks away, ignores me, and I go on pleading, can I go home now? Five minutes go by, twenty minutes, thirty minutes. They've forgotten me in the everlasting rush.

The DVDs pile up on the kitchen table, the childhood cartoons with the action movies and comedies. Paul's mother straightens them on the table while upstairs I'm making love, possibly. His mother calls us and Paul's belt buckle scrapes the wood floor, he swears shit shit shit, like me. In the living room she lays out her plan, she wants to pick up the DVD cabinet and take it out the back door, she wants it gone now. She says to me you take one end, I'll take the other and Paul says you take the right foot and I'll take the left. We go from the living room to the kitchen with the cabinet and then we have to go down ten steps, the veranda steps. With every step we go down we crack a joke. Paul's mother keeps her face closed, she says this won't work, it's not going to work. My fingers slip, I hold tight and we keep going, down the second step then the third, we're going to get rid of it but where will the DVDs go once the cabinet's in the yard, once there's that empty spot in the living room between his father's home theater and the overripe flower lamp?

This rush is not my problem, I want to leave and I say so to a colleague, waiting for her to agree, but she looks at me wide-eyed. Oh come on you're not going to leave now, you'll land us all in the shit. A team's got to hold together. I shoot back that I've been working beyond my scheduled time for an hour and her silence says it's been two hours for me, what do you want. She adds if you leave I'll be all alone on headset, I'll have to take orders and put them together too. In the end she anticipates my question, she who boasts of having worked in one of the chain's best restaurants, ranked fifth in productivity. Often the new girls look at her with dreamy eyes, beg her to tell them about it, what's it like there? Not like this place, I can tell you that much. She answers the question I haven't asked, looking away, worried that a manager might spot us, watching for a mana coming with her characteristic instinct.

—No one's coming in to help with the end of the rush tonight.

Paul's mother watches us creep along and says easy, easy, I think she hates me because she's seen my T-shirt's on backwards. She's wearing a floral blouse and sunglasses. Suntanned, she runs her fingers through her hair and her ring gets snagged so she takes it off and puts it down on the kitchen counter, in the middle of her jewels. Paul's mother likes to say no worries, not a problem, but she has more wrinkles around her eyes than my father. Every time we take a break she looks at us in silence.

On the fifth step she tells me forget it, it's not worth it, it's too complicated, forget it. She goes on just let it go, it'll fall to the bottom of the stairs and I'll take it to the dump. Paul stops, he says it's okay, this will work, we can make it. His mother shakes her head, no no you've got to forget it and her words lose their meaning. The DVD cabinet smells brand-new, my fingers cling to it. Paul goes down the sixth step, the Australian shepherd is watching us through the French door, curious. My wrists hurt but I hold on for all I'm worth. Will my father end up salvaging it from the dump? If he brings it home he'll put it in the garage next to the strollers, he'll polish it with a special compound. I stole it from the factory, they throw out a bunch of stuff like that, it's just like with batteries, you don't want to spread it around that you're helping yourself but it's going to the dump anyway so it's ours. Then my father will tell the whole family about it, whoever it was must not have wanted it anymore, they were moving, people will throw away anything nowadays. A cousin will protest, there's got to be a loose hinge, it's got to have a crack somewhere, but no, we tried to figure out what was wrong with it but it's brand new, it's the real thing, it just goes to show.

In the locker room, the thirty crew members' phones with their pill reminders have gradually stopped pinging, their memory's lost, put to sleep by the chain. You have to push a button to make the door open and it's raining outside. Under the awning the crew members talk about the *27 more pending*, gathering together as if after a lost battle. Around us, a field full of campers lies next to a shopping area too lit up for this hour of the night. The car's always parked in the same spot, the door slams and that's it.

I open the bag, the soda's popped open inside. I try to save the meal but it's too late. I end up putting the dripping food in my mouth and Radio Béton says it's midnight. I wipe my fingers on the paper bag, look at my garbage on the passenger seat, tempted to let it accumulate there, all the just-got-off-work garbage. A few palm trees are swaying in the rain. Further on, a bicycle's fallen in the middle of a roundabout, the wheel is spinning in the grass, the rider sitting a few yards away. His face lights up with the headlights of the passing cars and his arm goes up every time to protect him from the glare.

I release the emergency brake. The right blinker's stopped working, I drive the wrong way out of the parking lot, Radio Béton says we'll be right back with. I shift into third. I don't remember if I've washed my hands. After a moment, I take off the mask I still have on under my chin.

We get the cabinet onto the seventh step and Paul's mother yells that's enough! let it go! let it go! She's taken off her sunglasses, they're hanging from the neckline of her blouse and she takes her head in her hands. Paul steps away without a word, stops fighting it, now it's only my fingers that haven't given up, they're turning white. Paul looks at me and says that's enough now Claire, you can't hold it all by yourself, you've got to let go. Long-faced, brown-eyed, Paul is as tan as his mother but without her closed look, thanks to the braces on his teeth. The arch of his brace keeps his mouth partly open, he rubs the back of his neck with his scraped palm. His mother's back in the kitchen, she doesn't hear us. Standing in front of the DVDs, she says I can't believe this I can't believe this over and over again, her two hands joined in prayer, her forearms on the table. Her ring is still on the countertop, the dishwasher keeps going, the dog has disappeared.

The DVD cabinet is balanced in the middle of the staircase, suspended between two steps, and Paul's mother bursts into tears. Damn it why's everything so complicated? I can't take it, I can't take it. Paul wants to go to her but his father's DVD cabinet is in the middle of the stairway and he can't get by. There's only one solution but Paul doesn't say anything. He takes one last look at the doors of the cabinet, carefully taped shut. Little by little my fingers relax. Paul silently steps away and the cabinet slides down the steps, falls forward, somersaults, the sides are scratched by the banisters and it crash-lands at the bottom of the staircase.

✳ ✳ ✳

My father got his new coveralls the day I came home from boarding school for the weekend. You won't be seeing this again for a while, don't miss out kiddos. He takes them out of their plastic wrapper, carefully unfolds them like a precious gown from its silk paper and we become his models. Mama grabs the camera to take our pictures. She says smile and I close my mouth, I hide my teeth to mime arduous labor, work ethic, concentration. Hands on hips, chin back, I stand stoically in front of the couch, cleared off for the occasion. Mama says look at me and all I look at is my father behind her. I'm looking only at my father, as if to penetrate his mind, to be in his place for a moment, to lock a dead rabbit away in a computer tower and tick every box on the preventive maintenance checklist to get out of having to do a repair. Maintenance consists of avoiding disruption, preventing malfunction, and silently maintaining normal operations.

I'm thinking my father doesn't see me, his mind is on something else, I think, but I hold the pose, mama laughs, my toes are clenched in the safety shoes. I'm just about to say I don't want to play anymore when my father gets up and comes to me. Without a word, he puts his hardhat on my head. I'm still looking in the same direction, where my father was sitting. The hardhat's not enough for me. I want to go deeper into his character. He's crowned me, but I need more.

The next morning, I don't see my father leave the apartment, back out into the cold, and into the car where he tells himself it was a nice weekend. I don't need to see him, the cold's come under the door to my room. I smell his scent around the table when I eat my breakfast. He didn't clear away his bowl.

—You've got a real campground outside your drive-thru!

I see my colleague shrug. At the counter, a few yards away, I'm making up the orders for the delivery guys. Their bikes and scooters are parked all around the drive-thru. Sitting on folding chairs, they keep their delivery cubes at their feet. They've got music on, the volume goes up when the orders turn sparse. They're waiting for me to open the second window and shout the number of the order just up. No matter the number, they all come forward and one of them tells the others that's mine, that's mine, BB39 that's mine. He comes and picks it up. I wish him luck, often we both say it at the same time.

Sometimes I call and no one comes, so then I leave the bag on the windowsill and turn back toward the counter. Sometimes a driver gets mad and I have to reassure him, yes your order's on the screen, they're all on the screen! I tell them I'm not working the kitchen, they're just going to have to be patient. No AC03 isn't ready, you all tell me you've been waiting thirty minutes, but my screen says 300 seconds, so give it a rest. You have your order number? Not my problem if it's clipped to your motorcycle across the road. No number no order, that's coming from management, I don't like it any more than you do.

One day I hear a colleague speak the number calmly, without shouting, and the delivery guys all show up anyway. When my turn comes I shout, I can't help it, I call out DP24 as if I were calling the roll. A driver comes along, I say hello, DP24? The driver says hello, he shows me his phone, I read DP24, I say thank you and DP24 starts up his scooter. His GPS says continue straight ahead.

—They're here every day?

—Yes, they're waiting for their orders. We hand them off through another window.

—How much does a delivery guy make an hour?

—A pittance, to be honest with you, next to nothing.

—Just what I was thinking, it's slavery, that's what it is. Even you, it stinks, I'm sorry but it stinks.

The customer takes his bag, releases the emergency brake, drives off. Internet orders on the screen, somebody's ordered twenty-five packets of ketchup. I'm putting them in the bag one by one when someone knocks on the window. My colleague's not around, I take a chance and open up, finding myself face to face with a child in a T-shirt that hangs off his shoulders, who asks for a free packet of peanuts and a cup of water.

Jérôme scans his badge at ten till five and joins his colleagues to review the night gone by. They tell him about an electrical failure on a robot but nothing big, and after his workday there'll be nothing but the preventive stuff. Jérôme walks his night-shift colleagues to the time clock, see you guys. They laugh together, talk about the medals that have finally been stamped so they'll be able to hold them in their hands in a few days. The three men in red walk to the locker room, hardhats in hand, and Jérôme follows them without realizing what he's doing, he's too worn out.

His colleague for the morning is already busy on a press. Jérôme walks to the robot, fifteen minutes, that's what he complains about the most, the time he spends walking. Back

89

and forth all shift long, in his heavy shoes, sticking to the safety zone, through the din, the thumping presses, he doesn't know of another job like it. It's the slow wearing down that he dreads, more than any concrete danger with an impact he can gauge on the spot. The wearing down just settles in and drives him mad, there's no other way to say it, and in any case no one will understand. All the other workers are watching for danger from somewhere else, always from somewhere else.

For the broken-down robot you have to take the part, replace it, reestablish the circuit, you have to fiddle with it the way you know how to do, hold on to the one end and the other. Jérôme's feet hurt. He remembers the cherry picker the week before, it stopped fifty feet up and the two coworkers inside looked at each other. They'd gone up alone, with no one keeping an eye on them down below, and now no one could bring them down manually since no one could hear them calling. Fifty feet up, and the two of them looked at each other, nothing to do but jump, old Jéjé. So, in unison they jumped up and down to lower the bucket a little at a time, to bring the two men in red back to earth, all the while fearing it might break, what do you think the chances are it'll break?

Jérôme is holding the two ends, he wipes his forehead, he's not defusing a bomb, he's not stressed, he's cold and the sweat rolls down his forehead, fever. He tells himself he's caught the flu and then suddenly you didn't forget to shut off the power, did you? like when you change a light bulb, turn off the lamp, you didn't forget did you? He thinks of his friend who kept his wedding ring on and his finger flew off with it, and then the one who watched his legs getting crushed under a press. The current flows, 220 volts, runs through the cables and Jérôme's body, following the circuit, it's finally been reconnected.

—I couldn't care less that he doesn't have his order. At some point, if they don't know how to read and they screw up, that's not my fault, I'm not going to make another one! My colleague called out the number. Nobody came. She put the order down at the window and if the wrong person took it, that's not my fault, let them sort it out between themselves! If I don't make another one nobody will, you can count on that. No, that's it! Yeah, well, go ahead, threaten all you like, I don't care, I'm not making another one! Ask for your money back on the app, ask for your customer's money back but you're not getting another order!

Caro's gesticulating at the window. I could have said those same words, and for that matter maybe it's me railing at the window, maybe I'm the mean girl with the purple hair. I touch the splint I've had on my wrist ever since the sonogram. The screen showed a black liquid in my wrist, cola, and at the time clock a crew member noticed it, hey you've got a lump on your wrist too? Same with me, had it for two years. Caro's waving her arms this way and that, she's got the window, she knows she can close it, but the driver says he'll be waiting for her when she gets off, you'll see, bitch. Further on, at the other window, a customer is complaining about the wait and a colleague says she's not in the kitchen, it's nothing to do with her. Sure that he's got right on his side, the customer spits out Don't give me an explanation, just apologize, the customer's never wrong. Then she yells don't take that tone with me, I'm not your dog, for fuck's sake! and the customer throws hot fries in her face, and she runs away. The car roars off.

Caro closes the window on the deliverer's fingers and comes to stand in front of me, at the counter.

—I forbid you to serve him.

He yells, but with the noise from the presses, the radio, and the early morning hour nobody comes. Hunched over, limbs tingling, his hands stay clenched on the cables and there's no way to loosen them, no way to let go, since he can't feel them. You can't loosen what doesn't belong to you anymore. All he's got is his upper body and his heart, the heart's there, it's beating in time as the current flows, flows, flows. He yells, not hoping that someone will hear him, more to let out a little of the current, and his heart beating, he tells himself you've got yourself stuck boy, you're all jammed up, fuck. He tries to break free, to take back control of his body, a body whose purpose is to keep the robot working. He can lean back, but his hands won't let go of the cables, he puts all his strength into it, but nothing moves. His colleagues like to call him the gripper, they say that Jéjé, when he gets a grip on you you can't get your hand away, that bastard will hurt you.

Jérôme is getting worn down, he tells himself I'm going to pass out, I can't keep this up. The radio crackles, how long has he been there with the current coursing through him, he can't feel the feet that used to hurt so, he wishes he could feel his feet hurting again but there's only the heart, beating full speed, all the rest is numb and stiff, a foreign body. Then, bending over and without quite knowing how he manages to break loose, freeing one of his arms. As soon as one arm is clear everything suddenly falls away.

In the infirmary, the secretary says we'll have to put this down as a workplace accident, but he knows they'll pin it on him, he knows he could get himself fired for neglecting the safety protocols, so no, no, I'm fine, let's not worry about it. One of the bosses is there and insists on taking him home, like a schoolboy with a stomach ache. In the car, the boss never stops talking, trying to make the time go by. Fifteen minutes later, in front of the apartment building, before Jérôme gets out, the boss finally asks the question that from the start has been burning a hole in him, that was your fault, right?

On the grid, my first name is adrift between three different stations, café, fries, and front. Every box in the grid is filled, every crew member looks at the grid before they put on an apron, or a bow tie, or a hairnet, and I don't know which getup I'm supposed to put on today. My first name is written at the top of the grid, like it's in quarantine. A passing mana explains you're on backup at lunch today, you help out everywhere but particularly out front, and I've been told what I'll be doing for the next few hours.

In the entryway, four new girls are listening intently as Chouchou explains how to move a high chair. She assigns each girl a task, she's in good form, a cigarette between her fingers ready for her next break. The new girls disperse, casting anxious glances at the counter so they don't miss a tray, Chouchou's trained them well. Seeing me, she comes forward, delighted to explain that she absolutely can't do without me out front.

I don't answer, I go off to disinfect an order kiosk, but Chouchou hasn't finished her sentence, she's saved me the greeter station out front and a surprise to go with it. She holds out a headband attached to a visor.

The key doesn't turn in the lock, he just pushes the door open. Mama is making breakfast, and I'm still half-asleep. The sun is up, light's coming through the windows. Even if we don't know our father's schedule very well, seeing him standing on the doormat when we're just waking up isn't normal. He waits there, his face bright red, as if he'd got the wrong house.

Mama hurries to him, holds him up as they walk to their bedroom, and the door closes. Nico is eating a piece of buttered toast and I stay where I am, standing in the middle of the room. All we can hear from the bedroom are stifled sobs.

When the rush is over, Chouchou asks me to join her at a table in the dining room. An evaluation sheet is lying in front of her, she starts to explain the various points she's graded me on. I stay standing, a cloth in my hand, I go on wiping a tray no matter how she tries to get me to put it down, I loathe her.

Around us, the new girls are bringing out the last trays and taking advantage of their nearness to watch what's going on.

Behind the visor, a drop of sweat rolls down my nose and I decide to leave it. Seeing me so impassive, Chouchou cuts it short. So I wanted to congratulate you on these last few weeks out front, you did good work, you obey the health regulations, you're efficient in a rush, you know how to prioritize and guide the customer so I've given you 20 out of 20. At the beginning she was talking to the paper, but now she throws me a glance to observe my emotion, expressed by a few blinks that make the drop fall off the end of my nose. She goes on: you also know how to point out the most urgent tasks to the new girls, and I wanted to tell you I'm thinking of leaving soon, what would you say to taking my place? I'll let you think it over, leave your evaluation in the managers' office, but don't forget to sign it. It'd be a shame not to sign a 20 out of 20, and besides that comes with a raise, so congratulations again.

Maybe I've gone too long without answering. Chouchou interprets my silence, she sees a question in it, she wants to explain, you shouldn't have helped that delivery guy, you know. Between her clenched fingers I see her cigarette snap in two. I take off the visor to wipe my face and Chouchou realizes I'm not going to say anything. She lays a pen in the hollow of my hand to sign my evaluation.

I take a few steps and my body snaps into my crew member walk, those broad, decisive, mechanical strides that seem to take hold of you after a few weeks. Carrying my visor as if I were coming home from a hard-fought battle, I hold the evaluation between my fingertips, not sure if I'm taking that precaution because I don't want to rumple it. When I reach the door to the kitchens, I notice the new girls gathered around the greeter station. They eye my evaluation with envy. They all want to take their place at the counter, reach the drive-thru. They all want the boss to have confidence in them, to tell them lunch is going to be a madhouse today, but for the moment they're cleaning table numbers. They dream as they disinfect the bathroom.

The kitchen door closes behind me, and in the locker room I take off my shoe covers and start unbuttoning the white uniform blouse. My evaluation slips to the ground and lands in the pooled water.

AFTERWORD

Claire Baglin's moving, laconic, drily funny account of her summer job in a fast-food restaurant—juxtaposed with her father's years of work as a factory electrician—touches on a range of experiences that will be entirely familiar to an English-speaking reader, but also includes a number of cultural references that only a French reader will immediately grasp. In my notes below I try to at least minimally bridge this gap. All my most sincere thanks to Claire Baglin for answering many, many questions, and to Louise Gerbier for her careful reading of the manuscript and fine suggestions. Thanks, too, to Marigold Atkey and Barbara Epler for careful editing.

JORDAN STUMP

NOTES

24   "Tu m'oublieras"—"You'll Forget Me"—was a hit song in late 1998.

24– The reference is of course to Edith Piaf's 1951 classic,
25   "Padam padam." The two lines quoted from that song might be translated as "It's as if my whole past were playing out before my eyes" and "The melody that goes on."

38   These table markers tell servers where to bring a tray to waiting customers; this was a common practice during Covid, to avoid gatherings around the counter.

54   "I don't see that he's corrected the verb": The fireman is wondering whether to write *fais* (since he's the one giving her the hug) or *fait* (since he's referring to himself in the third person). The latter is correct, the former not at all illogical; French is full of such little traps for the unwary, often "tells" about a speaker's education.

57   The 1962 film *La Guerre des boutons* depicts a rivalry between gangs of rural children, at first playful and then not. André Treton—who played Lebrac, a lead character—made only one other movie, in 1963, before retiring from the cinema.

64   "Les démons de minuit" was a hit in the summer of 1986; further on, the boss is singing an older hit by Michel Polnareff, with the refrain "We'll all go to heaven." The *médaille du travail* is awarded by the French government to recognize exemplary job longevity.

86   Radio Béton is a local station in Tours.

New Directions Paperbooks—a partial listing

Adonis, Songs of Mihyar the Damascene

César Aira, Ghosts
   An Episode in the Life of a Landscape Painter

Ryunosuke Akutagawa, Kappa

Will Alexander, Refractive Africa

Osama Alomar, The Teeth of the Comb

Guillaume Apollinaire, Selected Writings

Jessica Au, Cold Enough for Snow

Paul Auster, The Red Notebook

Ingeborg Bachmann, Malina

Honoré de Balzac, Colonel Chabert

Djuna Barnes, Nightwood

Charles Baudelaire, The Flowers of Evil*

Bei Dao, City Gate, Open Up

Yevgenia Belorusets, Lucky Breaks

Rafael Bernal, His Name Was Death

Mei-Mei Berssenbrugge, Empathy

Max Blecher, Adventures in Immediate Irreality

Jorge Luis Borges, Labyrinths
   Seven Nights

Coral Bracho, Firefly Under the Tongue*

Kamau Brathwaite, Ancestors

Anne Carson, Glass, Irony & God
   Wrong Norma

Horacio Castellanos Moya, Senselessness

Camilo José Cela, Mazurka for Two Dead Men

Louis-Ferdinand Céline
   Death on the Installment Plan
   Journey to the End of the Night

Inger Christensen, alphabet

Julio Cortázar, Cronopios and Famas

Jonathan Creasy (ed.), Black Mountain Poems

Robert Creeley, If I Were Writing This

H.D., Selected Poems

Guy Davenport, 7 Greeks

Amparo Dávila, The Houseguest

Osamu Dazai, The Flowers of Buffoonery
   No Longer Human
   The Setting Sun

Anne de Marcken
   It Lasts Forever and Then It's Over

Helen DeWitt, The Last Samurai
   Some Trick

José Donoso, The Obscene Bird of Night

Robert Duncan, Selected Poems

Eça de Queirós, The Maias

Juan Emar, Yesterday

William Empson, 7 Types of Ambiguity

Mathias Énard, Compass

Shusaku Endo, Deep River

Jenny Erpenbeck, Go, Went, Gone
   Kairos

Lawrence Ferlinghetti
   A Coney Island of the Mind

Thalia Field, Personhood

F. Scott Fitzgerald, The Crack-Up

Rivka Galchen, Little Labors

Forrest Gander, Be With

Romain Gary, The Kites

Natalia Ginzburg, The Dry Heart

Henry Green, Concluding

Marlen Haushofer, The Wall

Victor Heringer, The Love of Singular Men

Felisberto Hernández, Piano Stories

Hermann Hesse, Siddhartha

Takashi Hiraide, The Guest Cat

Yoel Hoffmann, Moods

Susan Howe, My Emily Dickinson
   Concordance

Bohumil Hrabal, I Served the King of England

Qurratulain Hyder, River of Fire

Sonallah Ibrahim, That Smell

Rachel Ingalls, Mrs. Caliban

Christopher Isherwood, The Berlin Stories

Fleur Jaeggy, Sweet Days of Discipline

Alfred Jarry, Ubu Roi

B.S. Johnson, House Mother Normal

James Joyce, Stephen Hero

Franz Kafka, Amerika: The Man Who Disappeared

Yasunari Kawabata, Dandelions

Mieko Kanai, Mild Vertigo

John Keene, Counternarratives

Kim Hyesoon, Autobiography of Death

Heinrich von Kleist, Michael Kohlhaas

Taeko Kono, Toddler-Hunting

László Krasznahorkai, Satantango
   Seiobo There Below

Ágota Kristóf, The Illiterate

Eka Kurniawan, Beauty Is a Wound

Mme. de Lafayette, The Princess of Clèves

Lautréamont, Maldoror

Siegfried Lenz, The German Lesson

Alexander Lernet-Holenia, Count Luna

Denise Levertov, Selected Poems
Li Po, Selected Poems
Clarice Lispector, An Apprenticeship
The Hour of the Star
The Passion According to G. H.
Federico García Lorca, Selected Poems*
Nathaniel Mackey, Splay Anthem
Xavier de Maistre, Voyage Around My Room
Stéphane Mallarmé, Selected Poetry and Prose*
Javier Marías, Your Face Tomorrow (3 volumes)
Bernadette Mayer, Midwinter Day
Carson McCullers, The Member of the Wedding
Fernando Melchor, Hurricane Season
Paradais
Thomas Merton, New Seeds of Contemplation
The Way of Chuang Tzu
Henri Michaux, A Barbarian in Asia
Henry Miller, The Colossus of Maroussi
Big Sur & the Oranges of Hieronymus Bosch
Yukio Mishima, Confessions of a Mask
Death in Midsummer
Eugenio Montale, Selected Poems*
Vladimir Nabokov, Laughter in the Dark
Pablo Neruda, The Captain's Verses*
Love Poems*
Charles Olson, Selected Writings
George Oppen, New Collected Poems
Wilfred Owen, Collected Poems
Hiroko Oyamada, The Hole
José Emilio Pacheco, Battles in the Desert
Michael Palmer, Little Elegies for Sister Satan
Nicanor Parra, Antipoems*
Boris Pasternak, Safe Conduct
Octavio Paz, Poems of Octavio Paz
Victor Pelevin, Omon Ra
Fernando Pessoa
The Complete Works of Alberto Caeiro
Alejandra Pizarnik
Extracting the Stone of Madness
Robert Plunket, My Search for Warren Harding
Ezra Pound, The Cantos
New Selected Poems and Translations
Qian Zhongshu, Fortress Besieged
Raymond Queneau, Exercises in Style
Olga Ravn, The Employees
Herbert Read, The Green Child
Kenneth Rexroth, Selected Poems
Keith Ridgway, A Shock

Rainer Maria Rilke
Poems from the Book of Hours
Arthur Rimbaud, Illuminations*
A Season in Hell and The Drunken Boat*
Evelio Rosero, The Armies
Fran Ross, Oreo
Joseph Roth, The Emperor's Tomb
Raymond Roussel, Locus Solus
Ihara Saikaku, The Life of an Amorous Woman
Nathalie Sarraute, Tropisms
Jean-Paul Sartre, Nausea
Kathryn Scanlan, Kick the Latch
Delmore Schwartz
In Dreams Begin Responsibilities
W. G. Sebald, The Emigrants
The Rings of Saturn
Anne Serre, The Governesses
Patti Smith, Woolgathering
Stevie Smith, Best Poems
Novel on Yellow Paper
Gary Snyder, Turtle Island
Muriel Spark, The Driver's Seat
The Public Image
Maria Stepanova, In Memory of Memory
Wislawa Szymborska, How to Start Writing
Antonio Tabucchi, Pereira Maintains
Junichiro Tanizaki, The Maids
Yoko Tawada, The Emissary
Scattered All over the Earth
Dylan Thomas, A Child's Christmas in Wales
Collected Poems
Thuan, Chinatown
Rosemary Tonks, The Bloater
Tomas Tranströmer, The Great Enigma
Leonid Tsypkin, Summer in Baden-Baden
Tu Fu, Selected Poems
Elio Vittorini, Conversations in Sicily
Rosmarie Waldrop, The Nick of Time
Robert Walser, The Tanners
Eliot Weinberger, An Elemental Thing
Nineteen Ways of Looking at Wang Wei
Nathanael West, The Day of the Locust
Miss Lonelyhearts
Tennessee Williams, The Glass Menagerie
A Streetcar Named Desire
William Carlos Williams, Selected Poems
Alexis Wright, Praiseworthy
Louis Zukofsky, "A"

*BILINGUAL EDITION

For a complete listing, request a free catalog from New Directions, 80 8th Avenue, New York, NY 10011
or visit us online at ndbooks.com